Boone Brux

Other Books by Boone Brux

- **Bringer and the Bane Series**

  Shield of Fire – Book 1

  Kiss of the Betrayer – Book 2

  Chain of Illusions – Book 3

- **Paranormal Romance**

  Suddenly Beautiful

  Spellbound in Sleepy Hollow – A paranormal anthology

  Tall, Dark & Deadly Anthology- containing Shield of Fire (Book One of the Bringer and the Bane Series)

- **Contemporary Romance ~ The Wedding Favors Series**

  Bridesmaid Blues

  Random Acts of Marriage

  Properly Groomed

- **The Grim Reality Series**

  Styx & Stoned- Book 2

  Dead Spooky – A novella

  Death Times Two

This book is a work of fiction. Names, places, and incidents are the product of the author's imagination or are used fictitiously. Any resemblance to actual events, locales, or persons living or dead is coincidental.

boonebrux@boonebrux.com

Edited by Tina Winogrand
Cover Design by Jennifer Meyer & Hot Damn Designs

Print ISBN: 9781938601125
eBook ISBN: 9781626228504

This book is dedicated to my sister, Lisa. Though many miles separate us, you are always in my heart…and now my books.

Acknowledgments

I want to thank Sandy Shacklett for her fantastic title idea. I give all the credit for its creativity to her. Thanks to Jennifer Meyer, who created an absolutely stunning cover. I'm amazed every time I see one of your creations.

I'd also like to thank and praise my critique group, the Critwhores. You guys have continued to encourage me with this series and I'll be forever grateful.

Huge thanks go to my editor, Tina, for doing the hard work. I appreciate you so much.

CHAPTER ONE

Being a widow wasn't as glamorous as it sounded. Unless a person had the money to grieve properly—say in a tropical country, drowning in endless Mai Tais—it really kind of sucked.

I should know. I've been a widow for a year now. Twelve long months of clawing my way through each day. My name is Lisa Carron. I'm a thirty-five-year-old, single mother of three, and today is the one-year anniversary of my husband Jeff's death.

It was also a year ago, today I started letting my appearance slide. Grief will do that to you. Lay you low and drag you into dark places you never thought you'd go. In my case, it was carbs and elastic waistbands.

For the last year, my kids had come first, my depression last. Tasks like dressing and combing my hair took a back seat to more important activities, such as lying on the couch and staring at the ceiling, or scouring the cabinets for spilled chocolate chips. None of my pre-widow clothes fit anymore. Still, I hadn't been motivated to clear off my treadmill and fire that baby up.

One aspect of widowhood I had enjoyed was wearing black. I know that wasn't a thing anymore, unless you're an elderly lady from the old country, but I embraced it nonetheless—maybe a little too enthusiastically. Everything I owned was black.

I'd fallen into a rut and until a few days ago, when my daughter casually suggested I run a comb through my hair as to not scare the neighbor kids, I hadn't realized how far I'd sunk. That was my *Aha* moment. It was then I'd realized my kids had weathered the crisis of their father's death and emerged on the other side in far better shape than I had.

The revelation was bittersweet. I mean, kudos to me for being an awesome mom, but damn. My frizzy ponytail belonged on the backend of a horse, and my nails looked like I'd been buried alive and clawed my way out of the grave. In a word—I was a hot mess. What I needed was a long dip in Lake Lisa.

Determined to get my act together, I dropped off the spawn of my loins at my parents' house for the weekend. Once back home, I popped a cork on a bottle of Riesling, sat at the table, and planned two kid-free days. The excitement made me a little giddy—or maybe it was the wine—anyway, for the first time in a year, I sketched out a Saturday that was all about me.

That night I slept like a baby and when morning dawned, I rolled out of bed ready to face the day. A slight ache beat against the inside of my skull, but it was nothing a few aspirins hadn't cured. Plus, the Riesling had totally been worth it.

I showered and headed to the Holiday gas station near my friend Vella's hair salon. Getting my hair done was number two on my list. Buying my bucket of soda number one. The sugary nectar was the only legal substance I knew that gave me the sustained energy I needed to get through my day of errands—and sadly, the main reason I'd become a little fluffy.

Before I could shut off Omar, my ancient minivan, *The Hokie Pokie*, my mom's special ringtone, erupted in my purse. A million terrible scenarios sped through my mind. Fine, maybe I wasn't completely comfortable being away from my kids.

I flipped off the ignition and scrambled to find my phone. "Are the kids okay?"

"They're fine, sweetheart." Mom's placating voice soothed my panic back to a normal level. A small plane from the nearby airport buzzed over the car. “Where are you? I hear traffic. Are you running errands?”

Translation, did you get your big butt out of bed?

“Yes, I’m at the Holiday station near Merrill Field. I’m getting gas,” I lied, not needing the lecture on the hundred ways soda could kill me. “Did you need something?”

“It’s sixteen degrees out.” *Temperature update brought to you by my mother, the neighborhood weather monitor.* “Are you wearing your winter coat?”

“No, it’s not that cold.” Refusing to wear my parka until it hit zero had been something I’d done since I was a teenager—a personal affirmation that I was an Alaskan woman. Plus, it irritated the hell out of Mom, so I’d kept up the tradition. Childish, I know, but some days I just needed that win.

“You and that stupid habit. One day you’re going to catch your death.” Her heavy sigh hissed through the receiver. “Anyway, what do you have planned for today?”

“I’m on my way to Vella’s to get my hair cut.” Vella was my best friend and supreme ruler of all hairstylists in the universe. “Possibly my nails.”

“Oh good, you were starting to look like a mangy Cocker Spaniel. Have her hit those roots with a little color too. You’ll feel better.”

Translation, *she'd* feel better.

Having grown up with Mom's backhanded comments; I now ignored them—for the most part. I was secure in my frumpiness, and looked passably acceptable to be seen in public, though Bronte, my daughter, would argue that point.

"Mom, are you sure you're okay keeping the kids this weekend? I can get them after my hair appointment."

"Nonsense. We're making ghost sugar cookies for Halloween, and your father is pulling out his gun collection later."

In the background, I heard a collective cheer from my twin sons. "Are you nuts? Do not let the boys anywhere near those weapons."

"They're just show pieces, honey. The boys will be fine."

Show pieces my ass.

"Uh huh." My father was a retired cop and had an unhealthy obsession with firearms. But arguing with my mother was pointless. It was a sad state of affairs when a fifteen year old was the most responsible person in residence. "Could you put Bronte on the phone?"

Several seconds of silence passed until my daughter came on the line. "Yo."

"Hey, do me a favor and make sure the boys don't

touch Grandpa's guns."

She gave me her perfected annoyed teenager grunt. "How? They don't listen to me."

"You're clever. Figure something out." Bronte was more devious than both her brothers combined. It was a trait I stopped fighting and now used to my benefit. "If the boys come home unharmed, I'll buy you those hockey skates you want." Even though they weren't top of the line the skates would still set me back. But my kids' safety was worth it. "We'll get them after I pick you up Sunday."

"*Right* after you pick us up?"

"I promise." I couldn't waffle or she'd think I was bluffing. "Straight from grandma's house to the store."

She was silent for a few seconds, but I had her. She'd been asking for new hockey skates since last season. "I'll see what I can do."

"Thank you, sweetie. Tell Grandma I'll call her later. And hey…Mommy loves you."

Bronte made a gagging sound and ended the call. I smiled, knowing nobody would be going near my father's gun collection.

I dropped the phone into my purse and opened my van door. It squawked in protest, the loud kind that made everybody cringe and turn to stare. I kept meaning to have my dad look at it, but then I'd be subjected to my mother's endless affirmations on how to *bounce back* from losing Jeff. Like she knew anything about being a widow. Sure, it might seem like my dad was dead when he sat in his chair watching TV, but he's just quiet. I'm almost certain my mother hadn't drained *all* the life out of him—yet. So, I lived with judgmental looks and knowledge that one more thing in my life was falling apart.

The cold October wind swirled around me and slipped between the collar of my black polar fleece jacket and neck. Shivers rippled along my shoulders. I yanked the zipper up and walked to the front door, tilting my chin toward the sky. I hated when my breath flash froze the material of my jacket to my face. It was like getting a mini wax job, and considering the lack of attention I'd given my upper lip over the last year, I wasn't taking any chances.

I pulled open the glass door to the convenience store and held it for a large, bald guy with bad manners and a worse looking trench coat. His dark eyes darted to me and then away again. Hunched and limping, he slumped past without as much as a *thank you.* Rude bastard. Normally I would have graced him with one of my famous snarky comments, but the way he skulked past sent a serious case of the heebie-jeebies up my spine. Instead, I ignored him and headed for the soda machine.

Something about fountain pop made it better than

drinking it from a plastic bottle. Maybe there's more fizz, less sweetness. Maybe it's the straw. A lot of things taste better with a straw. That's not a proven scientific fact, just my personal opinion. Let's just say I have researched soda drinking over the years.

Mr. No Manners slinked past and around the back of the store to the refrigerated section. I focused on getting my jumbo beverage, not making eye contact with him. A cellophane wrapper crinkled behind me, drawing my attention. I glanced over my shoulder. The first thing I saw was firm, male buns. The man straightened and perused the artificial ingredients on a package of pastries.

I silently scoffed. From his trim physique and well-rounded tush, it was obvious this guy had never enjoyed the luscious processed goodness of a mass-made pastry. He was too fit—too outdoorsy looking, with his healthy glow and casually tousled brown hair. He definitely gave off an Alaskan man vibe—*I hike, compost, and brew my own beer from wild berries I picked myself.* Yeah, I knew the type well. People like him rarely bought anything that contained more than three ingredients, and those pastries were only eaten by hardcore junk-foodies. I never touched them myself. The texture reminded me of soggy florist foam, or crumbling sheet rock. Not that I've ever eaten either.

Still—I might have been a grieving widow but I

wasn't dead. After one more appreciative look at him, I returned my attention to filling the vat of soda.

As I slid my thumbs along the edge of the plastic lid to snap it onto the cup, a deep voice shouted, "Give me all your cash."

My head whipped toward the front of the convenience store. Mr. Bad Manners held a shotgun pointed directly at Doug and Roger, the mini-mart cashiers. Yeah, we were on a first name basis.

Like a heavy rock sinking into thick mud, the situation registered in my brain. *Holy crap, it was a fricken' holdup.*

My fingers dug into my soda cup, my eyes growing wide as paralyzing fear rushed through me. I think I stopped breathing, not wanting to draw the robber's attention. My first thought was of my kids. Things were finally getting back to normal. Well, as normal as they could be. No way was I going to attempt some adrenaline inspired hero crap that would no doubt get me killed.

From those thoughts of survival, my mind quickly jumped to the fact that I might be on the nightly news and probably should have dressed better. Random Thought Syndrome—I was one of its many sufferers.

The snack cake guy stood unmoving. It didn't appear any of us patrons were looking to be local heroes, or from the robber's crazed stare, a possible fatality.

Rock music from the local radio station filled the silence. I mentally urged Doug or Roger to start shoving cash into a bag, but neither moved. Unfortunately, it seemed I didn't possess Jedi mind powers.

"Money! Now!" Sweat trickled down the robber's stubbly face and he waved the shotgun at the boys. His head flicked several times to the side, as if he had a nervous tick. Nervous tick equaled itchy trigger finger as far as I was concerned.

"Don't shoot, sir," Doug finally said. He reached toward the cash register and punched a button. The till dinged and the drawer slid open. "I'm just gonna get a bag to put the money in, okay?"

Good move, Doug.

"Hurry up." The robber glanced around the store, his gaze lingering on me longer than I liked, before darting back to the cashier. "And don't trip the alarm."

Doug nodded. His hair, a substantial sandy blond fro with a huge comb sticking out the side, bounced up and down like a dandelion puff bobbing in the breeze. Plastic bags crackled as he attempted to work it free it from the pile. Cars sped along Glenn Highway beyond the large glass windows, completely oblivious to the ensuing robbery and the innocent patrons inside. My heart beat against my throat and my mouth went dry. Taking a sip of my soda was tempting but the scene with the tyrannosaurus rex from Jurassic Park kept playing in my mind.

Don't move. Don't even breathe. Maybe this monster wouldn't notice you.

Seconds ticked by and still Doug fumbled under the counter. I knew these two college guys weren't the brightest bulbs in the string of lights, but seriously, how hard was it to get a stupid grocery sack?

Doug crouched slightly, and when he straightened, he held a big ass revolver aimed at the bald guy.

Time seemed to slow.

Several things happen at once. The robber's eyes widened, comprehension that the cashier now sported some serious firepower dawning. His gun jerked up, and before I had time to drop to the floor, Doug pulled the trigger.

The revolver exploded, catapulting the criminal backward into the stand of chips. He slithered to the white tile floor in a cacophony of crumpling cellophane. The ringing in my ears ricocheted through my head and my feet seemed rooted in place. Nobody moved. We just stood there with our mouths hanging open.

I think I spoke for everyone in the mini-mart when I finally muttered, "Holy crap."

An aftershock of adrenaline surged through me. I

slung my soda aside and raced toward the robber. Hopefully he was injured and not dead. I'd had enough of death for a lifetime.

Mr. Snack Cake seemed to have the same idea and sprang into action. He barreled around the corner, shouting, but I was too amped up to make sense of his gibberish. I dropped and slid the last foot, stopping when my knees plowed into the robber's ribs.

The good-looking guy waved his arms at me. "Don't touch him!"

Too late. Sorry, but when I see a scraped elbow or somebody with a hole the size of a frozen pizza in their chest, my ninja paramedic skills kick into action. I pressed my fingers to the robber's neck, checking for a pulse. Nothing. My hands drifted across his chest, but there was no place to start compressions. Not that it would have helped. Doug's shot had hit the man dead center—no pun intended.

Mr. Snack Cake skidded to a stop beside me.

I glanced at him. "He's dead."

His eyes grew to the size of silver dollars. "I told you not to touch him."

Obviously, the sight of a corpse was completely freaking out this guy. Good thing I'd developed a rather unhealthy obsession with CSI shows after my husband died. I knew what to do. I looked over my shoulder at Doug. He still held the revolver, his hands shaking, and appeared to be in shock.

"Call 911." His eyes tracked to my face but I don't think he understood me. "Doug." I used his name, trying to snap him back to reality. "Put the gun down and call 911."

The weapon clattered to the floor and he fumbled for the phone. Using the dead guy's shoulder for leverage, I tried to push to a stand. The sensation of being pulled downward tugged on my arms. I struggled to my feet and tried again, but couldn't yank my hands off the robber.

Mr. Snack Cakes leapt over the body and gripped me around the chest. His hands locked directly between my boobs. Granted, this was the most action the girls had seen in over a year, and normally I would have been flattered, but I preferred to be groped more privately—with fewer dead people around.

"Hey, pal, mitts off the boobs." I fought against his hold but my hands remained glued to the dead guy.

"I told you not to touch him." He tugged, but I still couldn't straighten, or remove my palms from the robber's body.

What happened next was like trying to wipe sticky fingers with a paper napkin. No matter what, the napkin clung to me—just like the robber did.

I was still bent over, as if locked in a deadly game of

Twister, when the cute guy heaved himself back and finally dragged me free. I won't swear in public, but I'm almost positive he groped my boobs again.

I couldn't be certain because at the same time I heard a zipper-like rasp and found myself reeling backward. Mr. Snack Cake caught me before we both fell into a postcard stand. I'd barely righted myself when the dead guy's body lifted from the tile and hurtled toward me. I folded in on myself, bracing for impact. But instead of colliding, the mini-mart robber passed through me. Somebody screamed like a little girl—I'm pretty sure it was me.

The man holding me gripped my hands, curling them into fists. "Hold him, Lisa!"

Every instinct had me spinning to see where the robber had gone. Nothing made sense. Had I just imagined the man passing through me?

"He'll run if you let go," the cute guy said into my ear.

"Let go of what?"

That question was quickly answered as the robber snapped back through my body, slicing me with an icy chill that cut through my bones. A shudder rippled through me and my mind couldn't comprehend what I was seeing—Mr. Bad Manners.

His translucent body flickered, and a dark aura pulsed

around the form. I screamed again and attempted to violently shake off the good-looking guy's hold. I'm certain it was one of those spastic, hyperventilating convulsions. Not pretty, but I wasn't apologizing for my freak-out.

"Stop fighting me," Mr. Snack Cake yelled.

Yeah, right. Every survival instinct screamed for me to get away from the ghostly entity glaring at me. I dug my boots into the tile floor and pushed backward, but couldn't get traction. Any movement I made tugged the apparition of the bald guy with me. The darkness around the robber grew and enveloped me. His anger beat against me as if it was my own emotion. It invaded my personal space, choking off my breath and the scream hovering in my throat.

The ghost yanked against my hold, which disconnected his dark aura from me. I gasped, inhaling a lungful of air. Then he jerked again, yanking me forward. I stumbled over something and when I looked down I saw the mini-mart robber's body lying in the same place he'd fallen, except now a pool of dark blood seeped from under his back.

My gaze darted to the ghost attached to me and then down at his body. I screamed—again. I mean, I was all about the paranormal, but in a romantic way—fallen angels—sexy vampires—pretty much any immortal who wanted me to be the focus of his world—but not an angry ghost of a violent criminal.

The cute guy leaned in. "Whatever you do, don't let go of him."

Not that I could. My fingers ached from the living guy's grip, and my nails gouged my palms. He turned me toward the back of the store, which automatically dragged the apparition of the robber with us. "I'm taking her to the bathroom to get cleaned up and calmed down," he said to the boys. "Lock the doors until the police get here."

At this point, he frog-marched me and what I now believed was a ghost, toward the back of the mini-mart.

The apparition fought our every step. "Let me go, you stupid bitch."

Wow, harsh. Logic shrieked I shouldn't argue. I'd seen the Amityville Horror. No way did I want blood seeping out of the walls of my house. It was hard enough getting red wine stains off the carpet.

"Shut up, Leroy," the cute guy said.

That silenced the robber's ghost. Crap, were these two partners? Had I just become a criminal sandwich? Nausea rolled through me. Maybe if I puked on Snack Cake's fancy hiking boots, he'd let me go.

"How do you know my name?" The spirit stopped struggling. "You a cop?"

Cute guy lowered his voice so only we could hear. "You wish I was a cop."

Chills slithered down my spine at his tone. Who the hell was this guy? The darkness pulsing around Leroy's ghost intensified and my head started to swim. It felt as if he was sucking the life from me. Blackness crept around the edges of my vision.

Don't pass out. Don't pass out.

Damn it, I'd been determined to get my life on track. It looked like the first day of my new life might be my last.

We entered the bathroom. The smell of industrial cleaner filled my nose and the flickering fluorescent lights intensified my headache. He kicked the door closed, sealing us inside the white tiled tomb.

"My name is Nate."

I craned my neck to see if he was talking to me. "All right." *Nice to meet you* seemed a little inappropriate for the situation. "Listen Nate, you need to tell me what the hell is going on because I am seriously about to lose it."

"Let me get rid of him first, and then we'll talk." His voice softened, the creepy killer tone lessening.

"Get rid of him?" I scrunched my face and laced my words with my infamous sarcasm. "Where do you think he's going? We're in a frickin' bathroom of a mini-mart."

Me and my big mouth.

"Pick!" Nate waited a few seconds before shouting the word again. "Pick!"

"Pick?" What was I supposed to pick? The ghost or me? Life or death? My fingers ached from his crushing grip. I wiggled, trying to get away, but he continued to hold me in place. "I pick life. I want to live. Don't kill me."

"Me too," Leroy's ghost said.

"It's too late for you, Badder."

I didn't know who Badder was, but when Leroy began to fight me again, my keen sense of deduction kicked in, telling me it was the ghost. Several times he tried to jerk away, but kept rebounding like a rubber band. His arms passed through mine, cutting my bones with a searing cold. My head pounded, feeling like it was about to shatter. Any minute I was going to embark on a psychotic episode of epic proportion.

A bright, blue light suddenly appeared at the end of the bathroom near the toilet. All of us stopped struggling and stared as the sink disappeared behind the elongating glow. The light widened into a rectangle and the intensity dimmed. Breath caught in my throat when an actual door appeared, and then slid open. Leroy Badder's mouth sagged and his shoulders slumped. At least I wasn't the only one stunned by the sight. Nate, however, appeared perfectly calm, like an elevator arriving in the Holiday bathroom was a normal occurrence.

My attention drifted back to the far end of the

bathroom and the man standing on the other side of the door. At least I thought it was a man. Something about him didn't look completely human. Maybe it was his coal black eyes, or perhaps the tiny bumps protruding from the front of his skull that reminded me of horns. Despite what was certainly an unfortunate birth defect, the man's head was a perfect oval. A solid sheet of sable brown hair slicked along the top and sides like glossy frosting, and the creases in his black suit were so sharp they looked as if they could cut. Mafia attorney popped into my mind.

Beyond him the room glowed red. Not like those red-light bulbs hookers use to advertise their services, but more like a roaring fire burned nearby. My first impression? Modern Gates of Hell. But that would be ridiculous, right? I mean, I was standing in a mini-mart bathroom.

"I've got him, Pick."

Nate's words snapped me out of my trance. "That's Pick?"

"Yes." His gaze slid to mine and he lowered his voice. "Don't let him touch you."

Like that even had to be said. "Yeah, no problem."

I must have been in shock, because I should have been freaking out. It wasn't every day you saw an elevator to Hell in a convenience store bathroom. My life was hockey games and laundry, not…well, not whatever this was.

"Nate." Pick's voice carved through the tension like a hissing blade. "Punctual as usual." His gaze tracked to me and his thin lips pulled into a white, feral smile. "And who do we have here?"

This Pick character gave off a seriously eerie vibe.

"A new recruit," Nate said.

I had no idea if they were talking about me, and it didn't matter. At this point I was doing good not to pee myself.

The attorney guy pulled a clipboard from a file pocket mounted near the entrance and scanned an attached paper. "Leroy Badder?"

"Yes." Nate didn't move or release his hold on my hands. "He just robbed the convenience store—or tried to."

Pick ticked a mark on the clipboard and placed it back into the pocket. "You've been quite the troublemaker, Mr. Badder."

"Yeah, well, let me go and I'll show you just how bad I can be." Leroy tugged against my hold, pulling me toward the elevator.

Panic shot through me. Nate had specifically said to not let Pick touch me, and I had every intention of complying. Once again, I dug the thick heels of my boots against the slick tile floor, and lunged backward.

Nate's grip tightened and he leaned in, pressing his

mouth against my ear. "When I tell you to release him, let go."

"Gladly." Though I didn't know if my fingers would open after being crushed for so long.

Leroy shook his arms, which caused me to chomp down on my tongue. I bit back a string of name calling, most of which were less than flattering references to his mother.

"Now?" I shuffled my feet, trying to avoid Badder's stomping boots. Then the ghost braced his foot against my thigh and hauled backward. "Now?" I shouted.

"Now!" Nate's grip slid from my hands to my waist, holding me steady.

With the help of Leroy's thrashing, my fingers uncurled and released the ghost. Leroy hurled toward the open door, as if being sucked in by a giant vacuum, and tumbled into the elevator. He lay for a few seconds, looking around. When his gaze tracked downward, his eyes widened and his mouth rounded in a silent scream. Before he uttered a sound, Leroy dropped out of sight. The scene reminded me of the coyote on one of those Road Runner cartoons. Seconds later, the cry he hadn't voiced wafted up and out of the elevator to Hell.

Pick stood in the doorway, plucking invisible lint from his suit until Leroy's voice faded. I stumbled backward and out of Nate's hold, hitting the door. My fingers fumbled for the handle, but Nate flicked the deadbolt to *lock*.

"Let me out." My hands shook so badly I couldn't maneuver the latch back. I had no idea who or what Pick was or where Leroy Badder had disappeared. What I did know was that I wanted to be as far away from these guys as possible. I pointed. "I'm not going in there."

"Calm down." Nate grabbed my shoulders and spun me to face him. "You don't have to but we need to talk before the police get here."

I stared at him, not sure I trusted anything he said. My fingers curled around the handle of the door. No way was I dropping my defenses so this guy could toss me through the fiery Gates of Hell. Nate released me but kept his hands raised, gesturing for me to stay put. I didn't move—was unable to move.

He faced the elevator. "Our transaction is complete."

Pick tipped his head in acknowledgment and straightened. "Until next time."

With that, the door slid shut and compressed into a thin line of light, shrinking until it vanished completely. Nate walked to the other end of the bathroom. "It's over."

I didn't release my death-grip. "What was that? Who are you? Where did Leroy go?" My questions flowed like verbal diarrhea. "Am I dead?"

"You aren't dead, but Leroy is. That doorway was a

portal, and Pick is what's called a *porter*. He escorts souls to their appointed destination."

"Appointed destination? You mean Hell?"

Nate shrugged. "Not necessarily, but in most cases, yes."

"What do you mean, *in most cases*?"

He stared at me, his blue eyes never wavering from my face, but didn't answer.

"What are you?"

Nate took a deep breath and exhaled. "I'm a grim reaper. It's my job to get souls to the porters."

I didn't know whether to laugh or run screaming from the restroom. There wasn't enough liquor in the world to drown the images of the things I witnessed. Not enough soap to scrub away the feel of Leroy sticking to me. And there was no denying I might have completely lost my mind.

Nate cleared his throat. "And you're a grim reaper too."

Okay, I'd definitely lost my mind.

CHAPTER TWO

"Me a reaper? Very funny." I pointed my shaking finger at Nate. "Okay, I'm leaving now. You just stay there and…well, just stay there."

"Lisa."

That brought me up short. During our initial struggle with Leroy's ghost he'd called me *Lisa*. "How do you know my name?"

"I've been watching you for a while." He took a step toward me.

"Don't come any closer, stalker boy." I spazed and plastered my body against the door. My left hand fumbled in my coat pocket and I hauled out my deadly set of keys. "I will gouge your eyes out."

Nate looked up at the ceiling, his jaw clenching and unclenching. "I knew this was a mistake."

"What? Killing me in a public bathroom?" In an effort to back up my threat, I jabbed the pointy end of a key at him. "That would be a very big mistake. My dad used to be a cop."

"I told them you weren't cut out to be a reaper, but nobody listened to me."

"What do you mean not cut out to be a reaper?" Rational thought and action sometimes eluded me. Instead of going along with his assumption that I couldn't do the job, I rallied my bruised pride and foolishness. "If there was such a thing as a reaper, which there isn't, I'd be awesome at it. And for your information, I've got a black belt in Karate."

He shook his head. "No, you don't."

"How would you know?" Stupid question, he was a stalker after all.

"It's my job to know everything about the reapers in my zone."

"Okay." I shook my keys at him. "Then tell me about myself."

"You're thirty-five, a mother of three, and your husband died a year ago today."

"You could have Googled that." I pulled on the door handle and tried to flip the lock open, but it wouldn't move.

"I didn't." When he walked toward me I faced him, sliding to the corner, with my keys still held in attack mode.

"You've been on our radar for some time, but with your husband's death I didn't think it would be wise to approach you about being a grim reaper."

"Good plan, let's keep it like that." I reached for the handle again, but he slammed his foot in front of the door, preventing my escape. I glared at him. "As a matter of fact, let's never speak of it again."

With everything I'd just experienced, and now this guy claiming I was a reaper, it was just too much to take in.

"We need to talk about it, Lisa. Now that you've activated your powers, a decision needs to be made."

"Fine, I've decided to ignore my reaperness, you, and—" I made a circle with my hand, indicating the other end of the bathroom. "The whole paranormal shindig that may or may not have happened."

"I'm afraid it's not as simple as that." He ran his hand through his hair, giving it a messy appearance that made him even cuter. "You need to be informed before you make a decision."

"No, I really don't. I've made plenty of uninformed decisions. Turducken, skinny jeans, the fruit diet, all bad judgments, yet here I am, right as rain."

"This isn't the same as making a poor fashion choice. There are entities you have to report to now that you've reaped Leroy Badder."

"I did not reap Leroy Badder. He just—kind of—stuck to me."

Nate held his hands out to his side and gave me a look that said *duh*. "Same thing. You have to answer for it."

I narrowed my gaze, not completely understanding what he was trying to tell me. "Who are these entities? Like the Human Resource Department of reapers or bigger, like God or Satan?"

"We can't talk here. I'll explain things after we've dealt with the police."

"Do I look like an idiot?" I gave an unladylike snort. "I'm not discussing anything with you and I don't need you to *explain* things to me."

After my husband died, I'd struggled with my own mortality and the meaning of life. I'd gone to a dozen churches, looking for solace, read books on life-after-death, and searched for reasons why he died. Let's just say I have a tendency to immerse myself in my projects. Unfortunately, I was exactly the kind of person who would buy into this reaper crap, hoping for a higher meaning.

Before he replied somebody pounded on the door.

"Police, could you step out here please?"

Relief washed through me. I needed to get out of Hell's bathroom before I did something stupid, like enlisting in reaper boot camp, or signing my soul over to Satan.

"Coming officer."

Nate approached and covered my hand with one of his. "Take this and call me. We need to talk." He held out a business card. When I didn't take it, he slipped it into my jacket pocket. "I'll explain everything then."

I stared at him for a second, no clever retort coming to me. But neither did I tell him I wouldn't be calling. I pulled the door open and squeezed out, making sure not to brush against him. By the off chance he was the Angel of Death, I wanted to keep touching to a minimum.

The next hour was spent rehashing the details of the robbery. I did my best to stay as far from Nate as possible, but he kept glancing my way with his piercing blue eyes. Why were the cute ones always nutjobs—or grim reapers? As much as I wanted to, I couldn't dismiss the bizarre events that happened. No obvious explanation for Leroy's ghost, the Gates of Hell, or Pick popped into my head. Common sense told me revealing the bathroom incident to the police would not be in my best interest.

After the officer finished with me, I walked to Doug. The poor guy looked paler than usual. I'd been frequenting this particular Holiday for a year and had learned that Doug was a sweet, farm boy from Iowa, who came to Anchorage to study environmental science. I'd done my part to make sure the police knew he'd shot Leroy in self-defense.

"How you doing, Doug?"

His round hazel eyes slid to my face. "I killed a guy."

I leaned my hip against the counter. "Yes you did. Thanks for that."

His brow furrowed. "Thanks?"

"If you hadn't shot him, he would've shot you, and maybe the rest of us."

I wasn't sure if that was true. Perhaps if Doug hadn't tried to be a hero and handed over the cash, Leroy would have escaped with the money, leaving all of us unharmed. Or in my case, not a grim reaper—supposedly. But Badder was dead, and Doug would struggle with that the rest of his life. What harm would a few possible fibs do?

"Really?" The expression on his face nearly broke my heart. He appeared to be clinging to any thread that would lift the burden of snuffing out someone's life. "You're not just saying that?"

"Doug, you saved all our lives." I indicated the store with the sweep of my hand. "My kids have already lost one parent. Thanks to you they didn't lose me too."

His posture straightened. "Wow, I did that?"

I gave him a couple of pats on the shoulder. "You really did."

Roger approached, his brown eyes still wide with shock, and his normally tan skin on the ashen side. "You okay, Mrs. Carron?"

Roger was a native kid from a bush village called Dillingham. "I'm fine, Roger. How are you doing?"

"All right, I guess." He glanced over his shoulder at the police, and then back to us. "Can I tell you something?"

"Of course." I had that effect on people. Complete strangers routinely bared their souls to me in the checkout line. I always found it weird that people were willing to tell me intimate details of their lives. If only I could get my daughter to share a bit about her life.

"You know after Doug shot the robber?"

I nodded.

Roger swallowed hard. "I could have sworn I saw his ghost."

To cover my shock I play dumbed. "Who? Doug's ghost?"

"No." Roger's tongue darted out nervously to moisten his lips. "The gunman's ghost. It was only there for a few seconds, but faded when you went to the bathroom."

I kept my face passive. "Really?"

"Yeah, he was standing right in front of you and he looked really pissed."

Pissed was putting it mildly. I gave him a strained smile. "Whew, glad I didn't see him. I would have lost it big time."

Roger clutched his hands to his chest. "Do you think I'm crazy?"

"No." I shook my head. "I think some people are more susceptible to the spirit world."

That wasn't a lie. I'd always fancied myself sensitive to things like ghosts and haunted houses, whether it was a sense of being watched, or a feeling of foreboding when I walked into a room. If I really was a grim reaper, that might explain my experiences. Maybe Roger's native upbringing connected him to the spirit world. Heck, maybe he'd taken a hallucinogenic before work. Besides the robbery, I couldn't explain anything else that had happened.

"Well, I need to get going. Are you guys okay? Did you call the owner?" I asked.

"Yeah," Doug nodded. Through all the hoopla, his plastic comb had remained firmly in place at the side of his fro. "He's on his way."

"Maybe you'll get a bonus for preventing a robbery." They looked at each other, their eyes lighting at my mention of money. I smiled. "Mind if I grab a soda?"

Doug shook his head. "Take anything you want, Mrs. Carron. Anything."

"Thanks." I slipped between a police officer and the stand of postcards, trying to be as discreet as possible. If I could get my soda and leave, I wouldn't have to talk to crazy

Nate again.

I opted for the forty-four ounce jug and made a break for the front door. A cop still questioned him, but Nate glanced in my direction. Our gazes locked for a few seconds, and then he flicked his head toward me, indicating our business wasn't finished. I silently groaned. A slick ditch would have been too easy.

Despite the crowd gathered beyond the yellow police tape, I pushed open the glass door and stepped outside. Cameras clicked and questions were shouted at me, but I kept my head down and walked briskly to my van. Why couldn't the robbery have happened *after* I'd gotten my hair done?

I drove to the Northway Mall, where Vella's Star Power Salon resided. I parked, grabbed my soda and purse, and locked Omar. The brisk breeze registered, but the shivers running through me were not caused from the cold. I was still trying to wrap my head around everything, but not having much luck.

At least I'd be able to relay all the events to Vella. Her quirky outlook on life was one of acceptance and what-ifs. Hopefully, she wouldn't suggest I seek psychiatric help or up my meds—which I did not take. Vella thought everybody should be on *happy pills*, as she referred to them. Not me, I preferred to suffer through my pain.

The mall was quiet for a Saturday morning. Then again, it was usually quiet. Situated in the not so posh section of town, the stores in the Northway Mall came and went. There were a few steady merchants, and personally, I liked the smaller crowds. But I'm sure the storeowners would disagree.

The smell of hair color hung in the air and Elvis Presley crooned over the speaker system when I entered the salon. She was a diehard Elvis fan and even owned a motion activated, life-size cutout of him in her house. The damn thing scared me to death one night when I stayed with her. Stumbling down the dim hallway for a midnight pee, I'd passed her *Elvis room*. From out of the darkness I heard, "Thank you, thank you very much." When I screamed Vella's husband, Bud, ran out of their bedroom in his tidy whites, wielding a baseball bat. Let's just say there are things that can't be unseen.

"You're late." Vella lounged at her station, pawing through a celebrity magazine. "I thought you were going to be here at nine o'clock."

Vella was from Texas, and although she'd lived in the great north for over twenty years, she'd refused to relinquish her big bleached blond hair and tanning bed. I called her Menopause Barbie—not to her face.

I plopped down in the chair next to her. "I would

have but I got stuck in the middle of a mini-mart robbery."

"What?" She tossed her magazine onto the counter "Girl, are you okay?"

"Yeah, fine—well, physically fine." I sighed. "Which is more than I can say for Leroy Badder."

Vella shrugged. "Who's that?"

"The guy who robbed the store. You know Doug, the kid from Iowa?"

"Big hair?" Vella held her hands out to the sides of her head.

"Yeah, he shot and killed the guy." The memory of the blood seeping from under Leroy's body made me shudder. "It was awful."

"Sweet Jesus, and here I had my panties in a bunch, thinking you were having one of your pity parties."

If anybody other than my best friend had said that to me I would have ripped their head off. But when Jeff died, she'd been right beside me, holding my hand, wiping my tears, and taking care of my kids when I'd had too much.

"Hello ladies, and I use that term loosely." Jonathan, the salon's receptionist, sauntered in, carrying two large cups of coffee. "Decided to get out of bed, I see."

I growled at him and bared my teeth.

"Ooo, feisty. I like that." He handed Vella her coffee. "I figured you'd have your barrel of sugar water, so I didn't get you any coffee."

Jonathan was okay. He was the stereotypical gay guy, impeccably dressed, feminine demeanor, and knew all the latest gossip. The last quality made me wary when talking about my personal life. Spilling the details of the robbery around him guaranteed the story would be making the rounds in the rumor mill within the hour.

"Actually, I'd love a cup. Thank you." I needed to tell Vella about my slam dance with the paranormal world without him around. Pasting on my sweetest smile, I said. "Tall mocha, no whip. You're a treasure."

He gave an indignant grunt and looked to Vella for support.

"She was just in a robbery, Jonathan. The girl needs coffee."

His eyes widened. "Really? You were at the Holiday?"

Already he'd heard about the holdup? That was exactly why I wouldn't discuss my private life around him. "Yes, and I'll give you all the gory details when you get back—with my tall mocha."

"Oh goodie." He spun and headed out of the salon, his boot heels clicking across the tile floor.

"What's going on?" Vella took a drink of her coffee and narrowed her eyes. "I know you like to mess with

Jonathan, but I'm sensing there's something more to this."

I glanced over my shoulder to make sure he was gone, and then looked back at my friend. Qualifying my explanation first was more for my benefit than her. Why would she believe me when I barely believed it myself? "Hear me out before you pass judgment on my sanity."

Both of her perfectly sculpted and clipped eyebrows lifted. "Girl, you know I don't judge."

I refrained from commenting on that blatant lie. "After Leroy, the robber, was shot, I touched him to see if he was dead."

"Ick, did you wash your hands?"

I looked at my fingers. There should have been blood on them but there wasn't. "Yes," I lied. "Like I was saying, I checked to see if he was dead."

"Was he?"

"Sort of." I took a deep breath and plunged forward with my story. "When I stood, his spirit lifted out of his body and went right through me."

Vella shifted in her chair and crossed her legs, her focus zeroing in on me. "Go on."

The story rushed out like air from a balloon. When I was finished, I took a deep breath. "Nate gave me his card and said we needed to talk."

She tapped her long nail against the side of her cup.

"The Angel of Death has a business card?"

"I know, right? What kind of reaper doesn't carry a scythe, but has a business card?" I shook my head. "He's probably a weirdo stalker. The guy knew all sorts of shit about me. The whole thing was beyond peculiar."

"Well, I think it's safe to say this Nate is a little touched in the head." She took another drink and seemed to contemplate what I told her. The bubblegum pink nails of her other hand drummed against the arm of the chair, and she pursed her lips, squinting at me. "Can I see his card?"

I dug in my pocket and handed it to her.

"Grim Reaper Services. Well that's just stupid." She pointed to the lettering at the bottom with her thumb. "There's an address."

I tilted my head to get a better look. "4831 B—" I snatched the card from her and stared at the address I knew so well. "That's where Jeff used to work, but it's the General Resource Services building not Grim Reaper Services."

"All right, this is getting weirder than my Uncle Clem's lingerie collection."

I harrumphed. "I'm not even going to ask." Vella's family contained more freaks than a circus sideshow and her supply of stories was endless. "Am I supposed to believe death is renting office space from General Resources?"

"Look, both businesses have GRS as their initials."

Vella leaned back, giving me a look that said she'd formed her opinion. "This guy is bad news, no doubt about it?"

"What about Leroy Badder's ghost and the elevator to Hell?" How could she not think I was crazy when what I was asking was irrational? "I know what I saw."

"Maybe it was some of that post dramatic stress syndrome they're always talking about."

"You mean *post traumatic*?"

"Whatever." She jabbed a finger at me. "It hasn't been that long since Jeff died. Maybe this was your brain's way of coping with a life and death situation."

"I guess that's possible." I looked at the card again. Something very creepy was going on and I had a feeling I wasn't going to like whatever this Nate guy had in mind. "But Roger, one of the cashiers, said he thought he saw Leroy's ghost too."

"Mass hysteria." She set her coffee on the counter. "We used to see it all the time when the evangelist healers came to town. Everybody wailing, getting right with Jesus. One time my Aunt Edith said she and a bunch of her churchin' ladies saw the blessed mother sitting on the altar, eating a burrito." Vella made a drinking motion with her hand. "I think the old gals imbibed a little too much of the blood of Christ, if you know what I mean."

"Mass hysteria, you're probably right." I smiled,

trying to ignore my gut instinct that what happened, really *had* happened. "Hopefully I'll never see Nate again."

Vella sighed. "Too bad he was cute."

"What does that have to do with anything?"

"A cute guy gave you his number—I'm just sayin', too bad the cute ones are crazy."

"Yeah, just my luck." Not that I was in the market for a boyfriend or even a booty call. "Do you know he said I didn't have what it took to be a reaper?" His statement still grated, even if he was a psycho serial killer.

"That's because he's never seen you wield a weed whacker."

"Exactly." I grunted. "I'd make a freakin' awesome reaper."

"Damn straight." She stood and pulled the scrunchie from my hair and threaded her fingers through my limp locks. "It would be kind of neat, don't you think?"

She scraped her nails along my scalp and my eyes slid shut. "What would?"

"Being an Angel of Death." Her hands rested on my shoulders. "Helping people cross over."

I opened my eyes. "What happened to me didn't feel neat. It felt violent and sticky." She continued to massage my head, but the look on her face told me that brain of hers was conjuring up all sorts of scenarios. "What?"

She shrugged. "If you were a reaper, would you have wanted to help Jeff pass?"

"No." The word popped out of my mouth.

Her hands stopped and rested on top of my hair. "Why not?"

Why wouldn't I have wanted to help my husband pass? So many people would do anything for a chance to say goodbye. "Because when I found out that Jeff had been in a car accident, he was already dead. There was nothing I could do about it. If I'd known he was going to die and there was still nothing I could do about it—" I paused, my throat tightening at the thought. "I don't think I could handle that." I looked at her. "It's a burden I wouldn't want to bear."

She held my gaze in the mirror for a few seconds but didn't say anything more about death. "So, what are we doing today? Short and sassy? Platinum?"

"Manageable and get rid of the roots." I made a chopping gesture half way between my shoulders and chin. "Maybe a few inches off to clean it up, but I still want to be able to put it in a ponytail."

"Come on, let me do something daring."

I'd had enough of daring for one day. What I needed was safe. "Maybe next time."

She grumbled under her breath and spun my chair to face the back of the salon. "Your shampoo bowl awaits,

Milady."

Getting a new cut and color would make me feel better, but I had another worry now—like I needed that. Nate knew who I was, which probably meant he knew where I lived. It was one thing to have my safety put in question, but there were my kids to think about. A chill ran through me. Either he had lied to me to make contact, which wasn't good, or what Nate told me was true, and I was looking at a life-long sentence as the newest Angel of Death at Grim Reaper Services.

CHAPTER THREE

I left the salon with a slick new do and my scrunchie around my wrist. The change had been subtle, but I definitely felt better. On the drive home my mind replayed the events at the Holiday station. I wasn't sure I bought Vella's mass hysteria or post-traumatic stress explanations. In my gut I knew I hadn't imagined the whole thing. Something had happened. But no matter how hard I tried to cram the incident into a neatly defined compartment, it just didn't fit—and I *really* needed it to fit.

I turned onto my road. The section of Anchorage I lived in was what I referred to as *established.* Homes ranged from 1970's split-levels to newer duplexes and condos. My house was a well-worn, but sturdy, 1979 two-story, located on Resurrection Lane. Though the street was named after Resurrection Bay, the irony that I was trying to resurrect my life, not to mention the whole reaper thing, was not lost on me.

As I pulled into our driveway, I couldn't help but think all I needed was a few junk cars in the yard and a hound dog on the porch to complete my house's tired appearance. Home repairs had been low on my list of priorities, because of grief and limited funds. To say I'd been shocked when I found out how small Jeff's life insurance policy would be a gross understatement.

I'd yet to deal with the sense of betrayal I harbored about that. I mean, how much of a bitch would that make me to be pissed over money when I'd just lost my husband, and the kids, their father? Plus, I blamed myself for not being more involved in our finances—and a lot of other aspects of our life as a couple. Like I said, my self-esteem hit rock bottom and dwelling on what I could have done better would be like pouring lemon juice into a wound.

A fat raven sat on the railing of my front deck. Anchorage has the biggest ravens in the world. They were well fed from the Dumpsters and tourists, and were roughly the size of a Welsh Corgi. This bird must've frequented all the feeding hotspots. The way it stared at me, all harbinger of doomish, sent another wave of foreboding through me.

The grating squeak from my van door opening hadn't spooked the raven like I'd hoped. It just sat there, peering down at me. Even when I started up the front steps, it didn't fly away.

"Shoo." I waved my hand. Besides giving me the heebie-jeebies, I didn't want bird poop on my deck. Melting bird poo in the spring is beyond gross. I crept a few steps higher. "Go on."

The raven cocked its head and made a gurgling sound that reminded me of a telephone ringing. Its whole demeanor gave me the impression it was trying to talk to me. Then the bird looked to the sky. I followed its gaze and noticed five more ravens circling like black vultures.

Could things get any weirder?

When I rose to the second to the last step, the raven extended its wings, gurgled again, and took off. The sound of air against its blue-black feathers whooshed with each stroke as it lifted to join the circling murder. I jammed my key into the door and ducked inside before the scene turned into something out of a Hitchcock movie.

After slamming the door and locking it, I peeked out the curtains in my front living room. All six birds had settled in the bare branches of a tree across the street and sat silhouetted against the gray afternoon sky. Maybe it was my imagination, but the birds seemed to be staring at my house. I let the curtain fall into place and stepped back. My purse slid from my fingers and dropped to the floor. This day was too weird. Maybe if I ignored the ravens, they'd go away. Then again, maybe they were an omen of things to come.

I needed to get my mind off all the reaper madness and refocused on being productive. More than anything, I wanted a shower. Mainly to wash off the hair from my new cut, but also to scrub the feel of Leroy Badder from my hands—actually, my soul. The incident had left me with a greasy sensation that coated my being.

It took a good fifteen minutes of vigorous scouring with my loofa before deciding I'd cleansed as thoroughly as I could without dousing my body in bleach. Once out of the shower, I slicked my hair into a ponytail and put on my favorite sweatshirt. It had been a gift to my husband on his last birthday. *I'm sick of being my wife's arm candy* was printed in white letters on the front and Jeff had worn it around the house the day before he'd been killed.

For a long time I slept with the sweatshirt, inhaling the last remnants of his scent. It was the only way I'd been able to get to sleep. Over time his aroma faded and I'd taken to wearing it—every chance I got.

The shower hadn't completely washed away Leroy's essence, which made me antsy. Whenever I got like this I cleaned. From the state of my house, I hadn't been antsy in a very long time.

With the music cranked up, I hauled out my cleaning

supplies. Sadly, I had to dust those bottles off first. Starting in the bathroom, which was completely disgusting and bordering on a health hazard, I began swamping out the house. How had I not seen what a pigsty we lived in?

The hours passed and layers of dust, stacks of unattended mail, and piles of dirty laundry dwindled. At seven o'clock I stopped and surveyed the area. The place looked great. Then and there I vowed to never let the mess get away from me again. Talk is cheap when you're high on cleaning fluid fumes.

As I poured a celebratory glass of wine, my doorbell rang. Still reveling in my accomplishment, I didn't stop to consider who could be at my door. It wasn't uncommon for Don Burner, my playboy next-door neighbor, to stop by and see if I needed anything. He was a nice enough guy, but sort of icky in a *hey baby* kind of way.

I opened the door and froze. Nate stood on the other side. Before I could slam and lock the door, he pushed it open.

"Lisa, we have to talk."

"No, we don't! I just got my house clean," I said, as if that was a viable argument. I yanked on the handle, trying to wrench it from his grasp. "Things are finally getting back to normal. We don't need to talk."

"Yes, we do." He palmed my chest below my neck

and pushed me backward. "Now."

I stumbled, which gave him the break he needed. He stepped inside. I liked to think I was tough, but having a strange man barge into my home snuffed out that misconception. I tamped down my panic. Where was nosy Don when I needed him? Once inside, Nate closed the door.

"You can't just shove your way into my home." I wasn't sure how I would follow this argument. Though I hated to admit it, I didn't possess any stunning skills that could physically eject him from my house. If he was a killer, the best I could do were a few well-placed bitch-slaps before going down. "I could have you arrested."

"Yeah, but you won't." His gaze scanned the house. "You alone?"

"No." I fumbled for a lie. "My neighbor, Don, is fixing my bathroom sink."

"Would that be the same Don I just saw leaving with two young women."

Crap.

I grunted. "No, that was his twin brother, Jon."

Nate nodded. "Right."

Damn, I wish I were a better liar.

"You're not welcome here." He took a step forward and I slapped my hand against the wall, blocking his path with my arm. If he was a grim reaper maybe he couldn't enter my house until he was invited—like vampires. “Be gone.”

He smirked. “I’m not a vampire.”

“I know you’re not. There’s no such thing.” I rolled my eyes, trying to give the impression I hadn’t totally been thinking that. “What do you want?”

“Give me ten minutes. Then I’ll leave and never bother you again.”

It sounded too good to be true. “Never ever?”

“I promise.”

He didn’t do any kind of scout’s honor hand gesture, so I didn’t know if I could completely trust him. “Ten minutes.”

In that amount of time he could have me sliced up and vacuum-sealed, but what choice did I have. I spun and walked into my kitchen. The very idea that he being the grim reaper was the lesser of two evils made me want to laugh. Not in a *ha-ha, ironic, isn’t it* way. More like a, *things keep getting weirder* way.

His footsteps followed. I cursed myself. He would probably track dirt all over my sparkling floor. I scooped up my glass of wine and turned to face him. My upbringing forced me to offer him a drink. “Would you like a glass of wine?”

He held up a hand and shook his head. “No, thank

you."

Hmm, very polite—for a killer. I pulled out the chair and sat, indicating he should do the same. I took a sip of wine, wishing it were something stronger. "Okay, speak."

He lowered himself into the chair and propped his elbows on the table, leveling a stare at me. "You *are* a grim reaper."

"So you've said." I took another drink and set down my glass. "Are we done?"

"Hardly." He eased back and sized me up, his gaze narrowing. "All right then, you explain what happened at the Holiday station this morning."

I considered giving him Vella's explanation, but those reasons sounded even more ridiculous than reaping a soul. I decided to changed tactics. "Let me ask you this, why do you think I'm a reaper?"

"We recently lost one of our own and you came on our radar as the next reaper in line."

"Lost one of your own?" I didn't like the sound of that. "You mean one of your reapers died?"

He shifted in his chair. "Yes."

"That's a bit ironic isn't it, the Angel of Death dying?"

He shrugged. "We're mortal, tools for the greater good of mankind."

I refrained from telling him how much of a tool I thought he was. “Isn’t the grim reaper immortal?”

“You watch too many movies.”

That was true, but I didn’t confirm his statement. Our conversation was idiotic and yet a hundred questions demanded to be asked. That’s another problem. I had an unhealthy amount of morbid curiosity. “How did this reaper die?”

He took a deep breath and exhaled, giving me the impression he didn’t want to answer. “He was killed in a car accident.”

“Car accident?” Unease crept through me. Maybe it was the same ability I had to sense the paranormal, but his answer instantly put me on alert. “When?”

He reached up to massage the back of his neck and squinted at me. “A year ago.”

His answer hung in the air. I stared at him, physically feeling the silence pressing down on me. My mind grappled with what he had and hadn’t said. “You’re talking about Jeff…aren’t you?”

Several more seconds passed before he answered. “Yes.”

Whatever humor I’d found in the conversation vanished. “That’s not funny.”

“I know.” He leaned forward and pinned me with a

stare. “Jeff was my partner.”

“Jeff didn’t have a partner. He was an accounts manager for General Resource Services. He wore a tie and took his lunch to work.” My voice raised an octave. “He worked late and provided for his family. He didn’t reap souls.”

Nate shook his head. “I’m sorry, Lisa, but that’s not true. General Resource Services is a front for Grim Reaper Services.”

“No.” I slapped my hand on the table. “I’ve been in there. I’ve seen his office and people filling out applications.” I pointed a finger at him. “And never once have I seen you. You were not his partner.” What Nate was saying was asinine and impossible. My husband had been a good provider, a great father, and an okay husband. He sure as hell hadn’t been a grim reaper. “I don’t know why you’re doing this, but I want you to leave.”

Nate reached into his jacket pocket and pulled out two cards, tossing them onto the table. He flicked his head toward them. “Our identification badges.”

My hand shook when I reached for them. Nate and Jeff’s faces stared back at me from the laminated rectangles. GRS was printed in bold, black letters to the left. I flipped them over. A bar code and a bold line of numbers filled the backside. “This doesn’t prove anything.” I pitched them onto the table and glared at him. "You could've had those made anywhere."

"But I didn't." He slid another card across the table. "This is your temporary pass. It will get you onto the fourth floor."

I didn't pick it up, only glanced at it and then back at him. "I don't need that."

"You do if you're coming to GRS on Monday."

"I'm not going to GRS on Monday or any other day." I sounded convincing, but I'll admit my curiosity was trumping my disbelief. "I'm not interested in whatever little show and tell you have planned for me."

Nate picked up both identification cards and stood, leaving my temporary pass on the table. "Think about it. If you change your mind, be there at nine o'clock."

I remained seated. "I won't."

"We'll see." He headed for the door, stopping at the kitchen entrance. Without turning around he said, "I'm sorry about Jeff. He was a good partner."

I didn't reply and it seemed he didn't expect me to. The thud of the front door sounded, and his boots clomped down the stairs outside. With my interest piqued, I walked to the kitchen window to watch him climbed into a black Suburban.

"Figures." What other color vehicle would a reaper

drive?

As he pulled out of the driveway, the murder of ravens, still sitting in the tree across the street, rose and followed his rig. Another chill ran through me. I rubbed my arms and turned. The laminated card glared at me from across the room. Unable to squash my curiosity, I crept toward the table and slid back onto my chair, picking up my glass of wine. Nate's claim that I was a reaper had been bad enough. To find out Jeff had been his partner—well, that was almost too much to believe. Almost.

As much as I didn't want to admit it, Jeff being a grim reaper made a lot more sense than me being one. For a while I'd suspected him of having an affair. Late nights, business trips, and vague explanations of where he'd been had all smacked of another woman. But maybe it hadn't been an affair at all. Death didn't happen at convenient times. Maybe he and Nate had split shifts, took turns sending on souls. Maybe Jeff had worked the day shift so he could lead a fairly normal family life.

I picked up the temporary pass, trying to control the guilt and anger building inside me. I'd never confronted him about my suspicions. If I had, perhaps things would've been different between us.

Why hadn't he told me what he really did for a living? I already knew the answer. We'd grown apart after the twins were born. Raising three kids was a full-time job, and Jeff never seemed that interested in helping. Don't get me wrong, our distance wasn't completely his fault. I'd embraced motherhood and let being his wife sort of fall by the wayside. My mother had always taught me that was what a good mom did. If I'd been smart I would have taken a hard look at my parent's non-existent relationship.

I took a deep drink of wine and dropped the card. More questions filled my head and I wouldn't be able to put this mess behind me until I checked out GRS for myself. I was like that, too damn inquisitive for my own good.

I walked to the living room and flipped on the television. Nothing looked mind-numbing enough to hold my interest and make me forget about the bizarre twist my life had taken.

A day ago I'd been a grieving widow. Now I was a woman, who had discovered her husband might have been leading a double life. Usually, in cases like this, the average woman learned her husband had kept a mistress, or fathered a second family in Ohio, or spent their life savings on gambling. But not mine. Oh no, he had to be a frickin' Angel of Death. And to top it off, he somehow passed it on to me. It just figured.

CHAPTER FOUR

Thankfully I had twelve solid hours to process everything Nate told me. I wouldn't have been able to hide the fact I'd been told I was a grim reaper if I hadn't had a good night's sleep. After picking up the kids, we headed to the sports store to buy Bronte her hockey skates, and then back home for a quiet evening of pizza and mindless sitcoms. I'd glossed over being in the hold up at the Holiday station, and after a few hundred questions, the kids became absorbed in their assorted electronics and toys. By Monday morning I felt things were almost back to normal—almost.

"Who pooped and didn't flush it?" I stuck my head out of the bathroom and waited for an answer I knew wouldn't come. "I just cleaned this bathroom. The least you guys can do is flush!"

I trudged back to the toilet and stared at the offending

floater. Then I slammed the handle down. It wasn't logical to feel compassion for a turd, but the sense that my life was about to travel down the same swirling path, created a weird bond. I dropped the lid and shuffled to the sink. My hair still maintained its bouncy style after last night's shower, so I kept it down. After brushing my teeth and washing my face, I swiped on a layer of mascara and exited the bathroom.

"You're not leaving the house in that sweatshirt are you?" Bronte crossed her arms and gave me a look of teenage disapproval. "What is this, like the hundredth day in a row?"

"No, I'm not wearing this," I said, even though I'd totally been planning on doing exactly that. "And I washed it yesterday, so it's clean."

"I think it should say *I'm sick of being my husband's armpit candy,* instead."

"I'll have you know your father loved this sweatshirt."

Bronte snorted. "You should have buried him in it and done us all a favor."

"Oh, real nice." The tongue of a fifteen year old could be lethal. I'd learned to ignore most of her taciturn ways, chalking it up to hormones and coping mechanisms. That's what I told myself, anyway. "Are you ready to go?"

"I'm ready." She shoved a thumb over her shoulder

toward the boys' bedroom. "But you might want to hustle Thing One and Two along. They're having one of their secret meetings."

Secret meetings never boded well and were best headed off at the pass. The last time Breck and Bryce sequestered themselves, I found all their stuffed animals wearing blindfolds and lined up against my bay window. That wouldn't have been so disturbing, but all my steak knives were missing as well—it was during their circus phase.

I knocked on the door, hopefully disrupting yet another nefarious plan. "Let's go boys."

The two jumped when I spoke, confirming their guilt. I'd have to stay on my toes for the next few days.

"Coming, Mom." Bryce picked up his fifty-pound backpack and slipped it over his winter jacket. He's my little nerd, and never leaves the house with less than seven things to occupy him in the van.

Empty-handed, Breck headed for the door.

"Coat." I blocked his path so he couldn't get past. "Backpack, homework, lunchbox."

"Oh yeah." Breck trotted across the room and gathered all his items in one disorganized bundle. "Ready."

I smiled down at him. My twins were polar opposites. Bryce excelled academically and liked everything organized.

Breck was the class clown and a sports enthusiast. Rarely did he remember a coat or to brush his hair. His mischievousness kept me on twenty-four hour alert.

"Get in the van. We don't want to be late."

The boys thundered from the room. I followed, collecting my fleece jacket and purse, waiting to make sure the kids were out of the house. As I walked to the kitchen, I slipped on my coat and zipped it so Bronte wouldn't see I was still wearing the sweatshirt. From between the overdue phone and cable bill, I plucked the temporary pass Nate had given me, and shoved it into my coat pocket.

Though it was only a stiff piece of plastic, it weighed like a heavy stone. Maybe it was just my conscience. After Nate left, my guilt about believing Jeff had cheated had grown. For the rest of the weekend my mind conjured questions I couldn't answer. By Sunday night I solidified my decision to go to GRS Monday morning. At the very least, I'd be able to satisfy my curiosity and put this crazy reaper business behind me.

After dropping off Bronte at the high school and the boys at their elementary school for open gym time, I headed down Muldoon toward GRS. It was another gray, brisk day, which seemed appropriate for my mood. At a stoplight I watched the cars speed past, wondering if any of the drivers were grim reapers.

I caught myself. Did I actually believe I was a reaper, or that they even existed? I'd always liked the idea of angels escorting me to Heaven after I died. What I witnessed in the bathroom of the Holiday Station was about as far from that scenario as I could imagine.

The light turned green and I continued down Muldoon, which turned into Tudor. I've never understood the naming of roads in Anchorage. For no discernible reason, street names changed. L Street turned into Minnesota, which then turned into O'Malley farther down. I didn't know why and never asked. Maybe those who named the streets had so many great choices they wanted to use them all.

I slowed when I approached the parking lot to the GRS building. Omar fought my attempt to turn right. Yeah, I'm blaming my van. I veered into the left lane and whipped a U-turn. Staying in the right lane, I pulled into Starbucks and shut off the engine. I stared at Jeff's old work place. Any other time it was simply a reminder of where he'd worked. Now it loomed against the cloudy sky, ominous and forbidding. I squinted, trying to peer through the top floor windows, but couldn't see anything beyond the silver glass.

I glanced at the clock on my phone. There were still forty-five minutes before Nate expected me. The thought of a little more time calmed me slightly. As I got out of the van and walked toward the coffee shop, shivers skittered up my spine. Somebody was watching me. My eyes darted back toward the van, but the rest of the lot was empty. I did a sweep of the GRS building. Unless somebody stared at me from behind the mirrored windows, I couldn't locate anybody. Then I looked up and noticed a fat raven siting on the edge of the roof. My steps slowed. I'm no raven expert, but I swear it was the same bird that had perched on my porch railing a few days before. It gurgled at me, as if to confirm my unanswered question.

I stopped, waiting for the raven to do something other than make noises. To my surprise, it pecked once at something on the ledge and then took flight. It dove and I ducked to avoid being hit. With a downward pull of its wings, it soared upward. As it did, something fell from its beak.

The object landed with a metal clank and slid along the sidewalk to bump against the toe of my boot, but the bird continued its course toward downtown. I picked up the metal charm and examined it. A cold chill raced through me. It was a raven sitting on the handle of a scythe, the blade curling above its head.

The charm burned against the palm of my hand but I didn't think it was from the cold. It grew hotter. I pinched the clasp by my thumb and index finger and held it up to the light. Yep, it was definitely glowing.

When I got up this morning I'd been so confident I'd be able to put all this reaper craziness behind me. I guess that wasn't going to happen.

A knot formed in my stomach. Coffee suddenly sounded unappetizing. It was probably best to face my fears and get this over with. I took a deep breath, pocketed the charm, and walked back to my van.

There was no simple way to get across the street to the GRS building, so I drove to the nearest stop light, executed another U-turn, and headed back. This time I turned into the parking lot. Not giving myself a chance to chicken out, I grabbed my purse and strode to the front door.

The building was exactly as I remembered. Large glass doors led to a utilitarian foyer, which was empty at the moment. A wide hall lined with dark wood doors branched to the left. I'd taken a few steps toward the hall with the intention of examining the offices, when the elevator door to the right dinged open.

I jumped and spun to see Nate leaning against the back wall. "I wasn't sure you were going to show up."

"Neither was I." I shrugged, pretending all this wasn't completely freaking me out. "I think I'm early."

He exited the elevator with a knowing smile. Maybe I was easier to read than I thought. His gorgeous blue eyes leveled on me and I mentally cursed him for being even better looking today. Though loathe to admit it, I cared what he thought of me, and was happy I'd gotten my hair cut and attempted the minimal amount of makeup this morning. However, I should have taken Bronte's harsh suggestion and changed my shirt.

Nate held his hand out. "Do you have your pass?"

"Oh, yeah." I fumbled in my pocket and pulled out the card. The raven charm hooked on the edge and dropped on the floor. Before I could grab it, Nate bent and retrieved the charm. I held out my hand, not wanting him to examine it too closely. It was tough to rationalize the raven and its gift being a coincidence. "That's just something I found."

His eyebrows lifted and he dangled in front of me. "A little bird didn't happen to give this to you, did it?"

"Maybe." I snatched it from his fingers and shoved it back in my pocket. "It's nothing."

The grunt he issued spoke volumes, letting me know I couldn't be farther from the truth. I shoved the temporary pass at him.

He took it and smiled again, a little dimple appearing in his cheek. I had the overwhelming urge to slap the cuteness off his face for no better reason than the feeling inept every time I was around him.

"Come on." He walked toward the elevator. When I didn't move, he stopped and looked at me. "I promise it's just an elevator. Nothing more."

"Right." After what I'd seen in the Holiday bathroom, elevators had become my least favorite place. I followed him into the car, praising myself for my courage—or colossal stupidity. That was still to be determined. "So what happens now?"

Instead of answering, Nate slid my pass along the top of the panel and punched the fourth floor. He leaned against the bar. The doors slid shut, sealing us inside. When the elevator rose, my stomach lurched. Not wanting to look at Nate, I stared at the circles, on the panel, following their lighted path, waiting for his answer. Muffled music wafted from the hidden speakers in the ceiling.

Finally he said, "That depends on you."

I figured he'd say something like that. It was a goading statement that forced me to engage in the conversation. I did the same thing with Bronte. I'd bite. "How so?"

"Are you here because you're taking the fact that you're a grim reaper seriously, or is this about assuaging your guilt over Jeff?"

I stiffened. "I don't have any guilt over Jeff." Nate cocked his brow in a wordless retort. "Fine." I crossed my arms over my chest. "I might have thought he was cheating on me, and I might be slightly curious about the whole reaper gig, but that doesn't mean I believe *everything* you told me."

"Fair enough." The elevator slowed and gave a little hiccup when it came to a stop. "After your orientation, I think you'll be sufficiently convinced."

I bit back *we'll just see about that.*

The elevator doors slid open to reveal a long, black reception desk with a formidable looking woman sitting behind it. Her hair had impressive height and reminded me of my aunt Jean, who refused to give up her sixties hairstyle. When I was little I used to watch my aunt slick purple gel on a single curl at each side of her head, and secure them to her cheeks with pink tape. Then she would wrap her entire head in toilet paper. In the morning she'd exit the bedroom with a perfectly coiffured hairdo that stood up to any windstorm.

"Morning, Madge." I followed Nate to the desk. He rested an arm along the counter. "You're looking particularly lovely this morning."

Madge's smile was taut and didn't quite reach her eyes. "Aren't you the charmer?" Her gaze slid to me. "Lisa Carron?"

I nodded and inched forward.

Her eyes lingered on me a few seconds before she released a sigh heavily laced with forced acceptance. "Fill these out." She slapped a stack of papers on the counter.

"Don't forget to initial the bottom of each page or you won't be allowed into orientation."

I shoved the papers back to her. "I have no intention of attending orientation."

"That's what they all say, Sweetie." The woman smiled again, which looked more like a grimace, her eyes squinting behind glasses nearly as big as her head. "Humor me." She pointed toward a row of chairs against the wall. "Clipboards and pens are on the table."

With that, she spun her chair toward her computer, dismissing us. I picked up the papers and looked at Nate. "Are these a binding contract?"

"No." His hand slid around my arm, and he led me to the chairs. Tiny spindles of heat burrowed into my arm where he touched me. I ignored it. "But you can't get past Madge until you sign the privacy agreement." We sat and he handed me a pen from the neat arrangement in a cup. "Mainly, these say you're entering GRS of your own free will, without coercion, and you agree not to speak of what you see and learn today if you do not accept the position."

"Who would believe me?"

For the most part the papers said exactly what Nate had told me. Except for a few paragraphs of legal nerd talk, the agreement was straightforward and something I could live with. Once I left GRS today, I'd have no problem never mentioning the entire incident.

Ten minutes later, I'd finished filling out the forms and returned them to Madge. After a quick perusal, she tapped them into a neat pile and slammed a staple into the corner. "Welcome to GRS, Mrs. Carron."

I considered reiterating that I wouldn't be staying, but from her bored look, I could see she didn't give a crap. "Thank you."

"Come on." Nate stopped at a glass door and slid my pass along the key panel again. The lock released with a little click and he pushed the door open. Keyboard tapping and low conversations I couldn't make out hummed inside. "After you."

I stepped around him into what looked like a normal office setting. Cubicles filled the center of the room and long glassed-in conference rooms lined each end of the work area. The place looked identical to the offices on the first two floors where I thought Jeff had worked.

"Morning, Mr. Cramer." A chubby guy in a tight white shirt and a Harry Potter tie popped his head over the top of his wall. "New recruit?"

"Morning, Harold. This is Lisa." I started to say hello, but Nate placed his hand on my waist and guided me toward one of the conference rooms at the end of the cubicles. "She's undecided whether she wants to work for us, but I think I can persuade her."

Harold chuckled. "If anybody can, it's you, Mr. Cramer."

When we were out of earshot I said, "You and Harold got a bromance going?"

Nate scowled at me. "He's just a colleague."

"Seems more like a groupie." With a gentle shove, he pushed me into the room and shut the door. "Are you some kind of reaper rock star?"

He turned to face me. "Hardly, and Harold is not a groupie. He's a Wannabe."

"A what?"

"He wants to be a reaper, but he's not endowed with the Grim." Nate walked to a flat panel television and picked up the remote. "If you decide to come to the dark side, you'll be working with several Wannabes."

"Huh, that's interesting." I glanced at Harold's cubicle. He stared at me with the same longing I stared at bikinis with every spring. I want to wear one so badly but it was never going to happen.

"Have a seat." Nate pointed to a chair with the remote. "This film is a little dated, but it gives all the pertinent information you'll need to make a decision." He slid the clicker to me. "If you have any questions, pause the DVD and ask." Next, he pushed a pad of paper and a generic black pen at me. "You might want to take notes."

"All right." I retrieved the remote and settled back into the chair. "This should be interesting."

I didn't know what to expect, but a 1950's style infomercial was not it. The women in the film wore torturous shoes, and bras that could repel a missile attack. Their hairstyles reminded me of Madge's at the front desk, and I noticed all the women were stationed at the Wannabe cubicles.

I pointed to the television. "So—what—no women were reapers in the fifties?"

"There have been women reapers all through history. I told you the film was a little dated."

"A little? Since this video was made entire, empires have fallen. We've walked on the moon, and wised up about smoking in the work place." A thin smoky veil filled the cubicle area where the women were happily typing and smoking. My lungs hurt just watching them.

"Focus on what they're saying, not the actors." Nate sat in the chair directly opposite me.

I concentrated on the message and buried my feminist outrage. After a minute, I found myself absorbed in the narrator's explanation of GRS.

"Every reaper is a descendant of Charon, the Ferryman."

I paused the video and looked at Nate. "A descendant of Charon? The same Ferryman on the River Styx?"

Nate nodded. "Every few hundred years, Charon comes to the surface for a vacation. This usually results in one or two pregnancies."

"So, let me get this straight, Charon takes shore leave, knocks up a few women, and then goes back to his ferry?"

"Yeah, he's the ultimate sailor." He glanced at his watch. "As a matter of fact, it's about time for his next holiday."

I shook my head. "Remind me to stay as far away from him as possible."

I pressed play and settled back in my chair. I admit the reapers had a good system. They were divided into different groups—illness, children, war, natural causes, and violent crimes. I wondered what group I'd be in if I'd accepted the job.

Once you make the commitment to join the GRS team you will be given a bevy of tests, both physical and psychological.

I refrained from asking anything about the tests. I didn't think I wanted to know and the less knowledge the easier it would be to forget this crazy mess.

With support from your area's command central, you

will embark on a career that is not only monetarily rewarding, but a service to all mankind. Welcome to GRS.

The video ended. Nate walked to the television and shut off. “What do you think?”

“What did he mean by monetarily rewarding?” This piqued my interest. I’d never considered getting paid to reap souls, but Jeff got his paycheck from somewhere. His life insurance had barely carried us a year and my savings were nearly depleted. I’d been putting off getting a job so I could be there for the kids, but I couldn’t ignore the need for employment any longer. “Do we get paid for being grim reapers?”

“Yes.” Nate folded his hands on the table. “Plus, you get bonuses for quota.”

I eased forward in my chair, mimicking his posture. “What are we talking here—barista pay, or would I actually be able to support my family?”

The corners of Nate’s mouth quirked up in a *gotcha* kind of way. And as much as it irritated me to admit it, he had my interest. When I got pregnant with Bronte, I dropped out of college and never went back. At this point in my life the best I qualified for was an entry-level position in retail or a receptionist.

“You would definitely be able to support your family.” He paused. “Jeff did.”

I couldn't argue. We'd always had everything we needed—not everything we wanted, but who did nowadays? "How dangerous is it?"

Nate shrugged. "Not very dangerous for us. Mainly we deal with the weather or inconvenient locations. You won't be assigned to War. That's the most dangerous post."

His statement brought my reeling mind to a halt. The image of hundreds, sometimes thousands, of people killed in a single attack, and only a few reapers to dispatch their souls popped into my mind. "What happens if a soul isn't reaped?"

"Purgatory, ghosts, limbo—it depends on the life they lived and what they believed."

A knot formed in my stomach, obligation pressing on me. If I didn't reap, then who would? Even if I'd been chosen by some ancient accidental pregnancy, the task had fallen to me. What if it later fell to one or all of my kids? If I took the position I'd be able to help them adjust. Not to mention the money. Thoughts of a bright Christmas, and fixing my dollar-sucking pit of a house pulled me toward the decision I so vehemently resisted. I planned on leaving GRS today and never looking back. How quickly plans changed.

I gave a heavy sigh, praying I wouldn't regret this. "All right, I'm in."

CHAPTER FIVE

The expression on Nate's face was a cross between relief and disappointment. I knew he didn't think I'd make a good reaper. He'd made that perfectly clear at the Holiday station, but he'd done his job by recruiting me.

"Great." His tone was in direct opposition with his words. "Let's get the paperwork started."

I followed him out the door. All the Wannabes looked up when we exited. "Everybody, Lisa Carron will be taking Jeff Carron's place."

A few of the workers smiled and waved. There were even welcomes from Harold and a woman sitting in the front row, but I also noticed raised eyebrows at Nate's announcement. Obviously he wasn't the only one who questioned my abilities, which made me even more determined to succeed.

I gave a little wave, but didn't know what else to say. Nate headed toward a door I hadn't noticed at the other end of the room. We stepped through, sealing out the Wannabes' intense attention. Dark doors similar to those on the ground floor stretched down a wide hallway.

He stopped at the first office. "Morning, Nigel."

A crisp looking man in an argyle sweater vest and slicked back hair sat at an impeccably organized desk. "Good morning." His eyes drifted to me and back to Nate. "Mrs. Carron has accepted the position?"

"Yes, she has." I answered, irritated that Nigel talked as if I wasn't in the room.

His lips pinched together, his gaze cutting to me and back to his desk. Either this guy was a complete ass, or was in girl-panic mode. He opened the bottom drawer of his desk and pulled out a neatly compiled folder of papers.

"Lisa, this is Nigel Bottomzumpt. He will take care of your personnel paperwork. Workerman's Comp, leave requests, and your orientation packet."

"Nigel Bottomsup?" I asked, not sure I'd heard correctly.

"Bottomzumpt, Mrs. Carron. With a z-u-m-p-t."

Touchy. "Gotcha," I said.

"She'll need to fill out the usual forms, W-4, retirement package, life and medical benefits forms." He placed a black pen on top of the packet, and slid it across the desk. "You do have a beneficiary in case you die in the line of duty don't you?"

"To be honest, Nigel, since my husband died, I've tried not to think about the what-ifs of something happening to me." I termed it my coping strategy. Vella called it burying my head in the sand. From the way he stared at me it looked like my avoidance issues needed to be faced. "My kids will receive any money I have." Which, if I died tomorrow would keep them in mac and cheese for a month. "I'd like Vella Anderson to be the executor of whatever benefits I'd get from GRS."

Nigel furrowed his brow. "You don't have any living relatives that might be better?"

He asked the question in a way that told me he knew my parents were alive. Of course he would since Jeff had been a reaper. Nigel probably kept a spreadsheet on all the employees of GRS and their families.

"Yes, my parents and brother are alive, but I'd like my friend Vella to handle the money for my kids." It was an instantaneous decision and I really should have asked her permission. But I wanted Vella to raise the kids if I died. She didn't have any children of her own and my parents were old, well into their sixties. Not to mention, the fact my mother and I butted heads on every subject. My brother,

Bryan, could barely take care of himself, let alone three kids. If I let him raise the kids, they'd end up in juvenile court by the time they were sixteen. "Trust me, this is best, and if my status as being a reaper ever came out, Vella would be far more understanding than my parents."

Nigel glanced at Nate, as if asking his permission to allow it.

"Is there a problem?" My gaze bounced between the two of them.

"No," Nate said. "You have the right to choose whomever you want."

"Damn right I do." I wasn't sure why there was even a question.

Nigel's mouth tightened. "All right, then. Please print legibly."

I turned my attention to the forms, ignoring the sick feeling the thought of dying gave me. The questions were extensive, not the usual insurance or privacy forms. I'm not sure why they even bothered making me swear I wouldn't tell anybody. Couldn't the big bosses smite me with a single blow if I spill the beans on the super-secret reaper club?

My hand hovered over the page. I'd already told Vella about Nate and she'd ask again. Hopefully I wouldn't get us inadvertently added to the supernatural kill-list by telling her about my new job. After all, she'd need to know since she'd be raising my children.

It took about half an hour to fill out all the forms. My fingers cramped from writing on the tiny lines. "All done."

As I handed the packet back to Nigel, the cell phone on his desk started playing *Single Ladies* by Beyoncé.

His mouth thinned even more and he picked up the phone. "Excuse me."

My first thought was that Nigel had a sweetheart, but my suspicions were quickly extinguished.

"Hello." He spun his chair so the back faced us. I let my eyes travel over his spotless office. "Yes, I will pick it up on my way home." His words drifted over the top of the chair.

Hmm, did Nigel have a wife? That was hard to believe. I couldn't picture what kind of woman would fall for him. Maybe someone meek and mousey.

"No, Mother, the couple's yoga is tomorrow night."

Ewww!

I'm sorry, but doing couple's anything with a parent skeeved me out. I had to repress the urge to mimic gagging. My gaze cut to Nate, and by the sneer on his upper lip he also struggled with the ick factor.

Nigel's voice lowered to a whisper. "I got it, Mother. Now, goodbye."

When the call ended, he spun to face us and set the

phone back in its original spot. He opened the folder of forms I'd filled out, and thumbed through them. After a few minutes, he shut the file and looked up, giving me a smile that didn't reach his eyes. "Everything seems in order."

I sat there, waiting for more, but I guess he was finished talking. "Okay then. What next?"

"You'll need to get your pass." Nate smiled at Nigel. "As usual, thanks for your help."

Nigel smoothed his hands down the front of his vest. "You're welcome, Nate. It's always a pleasure dealing with employees who stick to protocol." He peered at me, his gaze almost accusatory. "Welcome to GRS, Mrs. Carron."

I didn't know why Nigel disliked me, but the man obviously didn't approve. Maybe he held with Nate's belief I'd suck as a reaper. "Thank you," I said. "Have fun with your mother at couple's yoga."

His gaze narrowed, as if trying to figure out if I was mocking him. Of course I was. That was my impulse reaction when somebody treated me like dog do-do he needed to scrape off the bottom of their shoe.

I followed Nate to the next office. A large, fortyish, Samoan woman, with skin the color of caramel and eyes the color steel, sat behind a long counter.

"Nate Cramer. Where have you been hiding yourself?" Her greeting was the direct opposite of what we'd received in Nigel's office. I instantly liked her. "I've missed you, Sugar Pie."

"You know how it is, Rosie, work—work—work." He walked to the counter and leaned on it. "But I'm back." He turned, gesturing me forward. "Rosie, this is Lisa Carron."

Her smile spread, showing off pearly teeth. The skin around her eyes crinkled. "Lisa." She took my hand. "Welcome. I'm so sorry about your husband."

"Thank you, Rosie." Warmth spread through my hand when she clutched it. The sensation sent a wave of calmness through me, giving me the impression there was more to her than just being the office help. I made a mental note to ask Nate about the workers. Sure they were Wannabes, but what made them qualified to work at GRS. "I'm happy to be here."

She released me and pointed to a blue screen. "Why don't you stand over there and I'll immortalize that pretty face of yours on a GRS pass."

That comment endeared her to me even more, and I did as she asked. The thought of having my own access card gave me a little thrill. It had been a long time since I'd been anything other than Jeff's wife, or the kids' mother. Discovering that reapers really existed overshadowed the fact that I was now gainfully employed.

I let my arms hang at my side. "Should I smile or not smile."

"You should definitely smile, Sugar." Rosie wrinkled her nose. "Why don't you take your jacket off?"

I hesitated, once again cursing myself for wearing Jeff's sweatshirt. "I think I'll leave it on, if that's okay."

She shrugged. "Suit yourself."

Adjusting the lens of the mounted camera at me, she said, "Say *grim reaper*."

I laughed and she snapped the picture.

"Perfect." Rosie moved to her computer. "It will be just a minute." She tapped on the keys. "Nigel has already got your information in the system."

"We only left his office two minutes ago," I said.

"That's our Nigel." The way Rosie said his name made me think that maybe she had the hots for him.

I tried to imagine the two of them together, but couldn't quite make that love match. The whirr of a machine behind the counter started. After another minute, Rosie handed me my very own GRS access card. It was still warm from the laminating machine, so I held it around the edges and marveled at my picture.

My smiling face beamed back. It was the happiest I'd looked in over a year. "Thank you."

"You're welcome, Sugar."

"All right." Nate straightened away from the counter. "Rosie, as always you've brightened my day."

"You're such a sweet talker." She waved a hand at him, her laughter filling the office. "Lisa, don't let this silver-tongued devil talk *you* into anything dangerous."

The mention of danger popped my bubble of joy. The way she had said *you,* made me wonder just how many people Nate had coerced into hazardous situations. Had Jeff been one of them? "I sure won't, Rosie."

"Come on." He indicated the door. "On to payroll."

Money, now that was a subject I could sink my teeth into. It was the only reason I'd taken this job—well, that, and the niggle of universal obligation. I trailed Nate. "So what kind of pay are we talking about—you know, just a ballpark figure?"

"I'll let Willow fill you in on all the details." He stopped at the next door. "She'll be able to answer any questions you have."

Willow was a typical Alaskan name. We also had a lot of Ravens, Denalis, and Auroras in the state. More than likely Willow was young with the kind of natural beauty that looked like she'd been skiing over the weekend. I walked into the office and realized I was partially right.

She glanced up from her desk and gave us a super model smile. Green, almond-shaped eyes were accentuated by her long red hair, which was pinned up in a messy up-do. If I tried to pull off that hairstyle, it would look like I'd been wrestling a chimpanzee all night.

"Good morning." She stood and held out her hand. "You must be Lisa Carron."

It appeared everybody at GRS knew about me. I accepted her greeting. "Yes, and you must be Willow."

She released my hand. "That's me, or Money Bags as everybody calls me behind my back."

Nate sat in one of the chairs in front of her desk. "That's not what I call you behind your back." He smiled and folded his hands across his stomach. "Or to your face."

She lifted a brow at him. "Always a charmer, Nate."

Though Rosie had basically said the same thing, Willow's tone was not complementary. Obviously these two didn't get along. I sat, wondering about the couple's history.

"I think I can correctly assume that you've taken the position here at GRS?" She opened a file lying on her desk but her gaze never left me.

I exhaled. "Against my better judgment, yes, but I need a job."

Her smile was sweet and understanding. Despite Nate's problems with Willow, I liked her. "I understand your hesitance, but I'm sure you'll do fine." She paused. "I'm sorry about your husband. All this must have come as quite a shock."

"Thank you. Yes, I'm still reeling a bit, but I'm glad I found out."

I really wasn't. But, many times during my life I hadn't gotten the memo from the big guy upstairs. In order to cope with all the changes, I needed to believe there was a higher purpose in me becoming a reaper.

"All right, let's dive in." She placed her hands on top of the file. "GRS is set up on a pay scale that takes into account time in service and rank."

"Rank?" I asked.

"Yes, you will start out as a Deputy or a GR1." She slid the top sheet of paper toward me and pointed to a graph. "This is the pay to start with. After your six-month training period, you'll move up to a Deputy GR2. This will increase your income $112 per pay period."

It was difficult to disguise my disappointment over my base pay. The amount would barely be enough to cover our expenses. I nodded and studied the graph, not trusting that my frustration wouldn't leak out. Instead I looked at Nate. "What are you?"

"Lieutenant GR6."

I scanned down the table. His pay was impressive, about three thousand dollars more a month than I would be making. "What rank was Jeff?"

He was quiet for a few seconds. "Sargent GR6."

I bit the inside of my cheek to stop myself from asking more questions. There was no way my husband had made as much as the chart said. Or if he had, he didn't spend it on the family. That led to the question, where the hell had all the money gone?

"I know it doesn't seem like much, especially since you were used to Jeff's salary."

"No, actually it's fine." *Because I was never used to his frickin' salary.*

Not commenting further about Jeff's pay, she pointed to the next chart down. "But we also give you a stipend each month for working in a remote location."

My spirits lifted slightly at the extra four hundred dollars, but I had to push away the idea there was more money Jeff hadn't brought home. I refocused on my present situation. "Anchorage is considered remote?"

Her brow furrowed and she looked at Nate. "I'd assumed Nate had briefed you on all the specifics of the job and your duties before having you accept the position."

Now I looked—well glared—at him. "No, he didn't."

She sighed. "Anchorage is not considered remote, but the outlying villages are. You will be required to travel for GRS, and reap souls whenever needed."

"That presents a tiny problem considering I'm a

single mother of three. I can't just drop everything and fly out to Barrow or Dillingham. What am I supposed to do with my kids?"

"That's precisely why I expected this to be explained prior to your signing." She scowled at Nate again, but he seemed unrepentant. We were definitely going to have a few words after my orientation. "Fortunately, GRS has in-home care for those who need it or we will supplement your sitting costs if you have someone you trust."

I nodded. "I'll have to think about this. I can't leave my kids with just anybody." *Specifically my mother.*

Mom would take them in a heartbeat, but I'd be indebted to her forever. Still, I needed a job, and making that sacrifice would be worth it. On the flip side of the coin, if none of my kids became reapers, which I dearly hoped, then I wouldn't be able to throw my martyrdom back in their faces when they blamed me for their horrible lives. I was looking at the big picture here.

"Let me know if you need any help setting things up. I can introduce you to our caregivers. They are ready at a moment's notice and might be good to keep as a backup."

"Thank you, Willow, I really appreciate that." I liked her more and more. She and Rosie were the first people at GRS who actually seemed human. "Do you have kids?"

"No." She picked up her pen and tapped it on the

desk. “But I raised my sister—until she died a few years ago.”

Instantly tears burned at the back of my eyes. I swallowed hard, reaching across the desk to cover her hand with mine. “I’m so sorry.”

From experience, I knew nothing more needed to be said. After Jeff died people tried to console me by relating a story about someone they’d lost. Although they attempted to find a common ground and connect with me, I got so tired of trying to make *them* feel better. I ceased being the griever and became the comforter. It was very draining.

“Thank you,” she said.

I pulled my hand back and fumbled for a way to get back on topic. “I think meeting GRS’s caregivers is a good idea.”

“Great, I will set that up for us in a few weeks, after you get settled.” Her smile returned. “Now, onto bonuses.”

“I like the sound of that.” I glanced at Nate. For whatever reason, he didn’t seem happy. Maybe he and Willow had dated, and she’d dumped his grumpy butt. I added that to my list of questions for him.

“After every twenty reaps you will receive a thousand dollar bonus. On your hundredth reap you will receive an incentive bonus of five thousand dollars.” She slid another sheet to me. “This is the breakdown beyond that.”

"Wow." I glanced at the figures. "Twenty five thousand for a thousand reaps?"

"We've only had one person in Alaska receive that bonus." Her eyes cut to Nate and back to me. "But all the reaps were not harvested in Alaska."

He crossed his arms and continued to glare at Willow. I refrained from asking him how he reaped a thousand souls. Mainly because I didn't want to know, figuring it was a horrific natural disaster, or something even more gruesome. At this point ignorance was bliss.

"All righty then," I said, trying to talk past the uncomfortable tension zinging between them. "How often do we get paid?"

Willow relaxed against her chair. "Every two weeks. We do direct deposit. We're a paperless office whenever possible."

"Recycle, reuse, and reap?" I asked.

She smiled again. "I like that motto. We might have to adopt it for our conservation program."

Nate stood. "Is that all?"

Willow didn't look at him, but stood and held out her hand again. "It was great meeting you, Lisa. Let me know if you have any questions."

"Thank you, I will." I shook her hand.

"I hope you like it here. I'm sure you'll be a great

asset to GRS."

"Finally, somebody with vision."

Nate harrumphed and left without waiting. "Is he always like this?"

"Oh no, just around me." She sighed. "I'm sure he'll be somewhat human with you."

"One can only hope." I gave her a consoling smile and left. Something had definitely happened between him and Willow. Call me an office gossip, but I was already devising a plan to squeeze that info out of him. I skipped a few steps to catch up with him. "What's next?"

"Time to find out if you're pregnant."

CHAPTER SIX

I skidded to a stop. "Excuse me?"

Nate turned to face me. "Your medical exam is next."

"Oh." I started walking again. The only way I'd be pregnant was through an immaculate conception, which I was beginning to believe could actually happen. Who knew which of the things I once considered fantasy could possibly be true. "You're not going to be in my exam with me, are you?"

He stopped at a glass door. A metal sign engraved with *medical office* hung beside it. "Thankfully, no."

Thankfully indeed. "Are we finished after this?"

Nate checked his watch. "I'll come back and in about an hour. We can catch some lunch after that." His eyes did a quick track up and down my body. "You must be getting hungry."

Wow, he'd so effortlessly insulted me with his

judgmental scan. I had questions for him about the job, so I bit back my retort and plastered on a smile. "Sounds great."

Without any more discussion, because seriously, my self-esteem had already taken a beating today, I entered the office and shut the door in his face.

Cherry wood and rich plum walls decorated the outer lobby. The warm mood directly contradicted the utilitarian world that existed beyond the door. I prayed the doctor was a woman. Of all the employees I'd met so far, women seemed to be the only ones with an ounce of compassion.

I walked to the counter and tapped the bell. A feminine voice answered from somewhere beyond my sight. "I'll be with you in a second."

So far so good. At least the nurse or receptionist was a woman. Another minute passed, and the doctor finally appeared. She was around fifty and had black hair with two thick streaks of white racing down each side, as if they'd been painted on.

"Hi, I'm Dr. Jensen, but call me Candace." She held open the door with her hip and extended her hand. "You must be Lisa."

"That's me, the new recruit." I gave her hand a quick shake, relief washing through me. I didn't know how far up into my sweet junk she was going to get, but I felt much more comfortable discussing my girl problems with a female doctor. “Nice to meet you.”

“Come on back.” She led me to the first room on the right, and pulled a file from the pocket next to the door. “I’ll need to get some history before we start the exam.”

“Great.” I plopped down in a plum colored chair that was incredibly comfortable and would look fantastic in my living room. She took her place at a small writing desk. “Doesn’t a nurse usually do this part of the exam?”

“I’m the doctor, nurse, receptionist, and sometimes janitor.” She looked up from the file and smiled. “Besides new recruits, and the annual medical exam on the employees, I don’t see a lot of action here.” She shrugged. “I used to be an ER doctor in Detroit. I loved it for a while, but the constant crisis tends to take its toll. Here there’s rarely any drama and a lot of my day is free to work on other projects.”

“Sounds like a dream job. I’d like getting paid big bucks and having everybody basically leave me alone.”

“That surprises me. Most reapers like to be in the thick of things.”

I held out my arms to the side. “Do I look like your typical reaper? I have three kids, one of them being a teenage girl. The most excitement I’ve had over the past year was the convenience store robbery that landed me here.”

“Yes, I heard about that.” Thick black lashes framed her dark blue eyes. “I think you’re the first recruit I’ve had who accidentally became a reaper."

I sighed. "Once you get to know me you'll see how fitting my initiation was."

She laughed. "I'm sure you'll be a great reaper."

I grimaced and shook my head. "You're either being incredibly diplomatic or gullible."

"Between you and me I think the reapers could use a little more estrogen on their team." She tucked a hank of thick hair behind her ear and looked at the chart. "It seems to me reaping should be handled with finesse and compassion, instead of acting as if they're tossing a log on the fire."

"Oh, you've met Nate then?"

She laughed again and nodded, but made no further comment on the subject. "So, first question. Are you pregnant, or is there a possibility of being pregnant?"

Several answers popped into my head but I refrained from saying them. "No."

"Do you have any old injuries that are giving you problems or periodically act up?"

"Well, I sprained my ankle in a horrible gardening accident last year."

She looked up, her brows lifted. "A horrible gardening accident?"

"I was talking on the phone and carrying a potted tomato plant out my front door, when I tripped and fell." It had been awful and humiliating. Repeating the sordid details again dredged up what a Mrs. Magoo I could be. “I landed on the pot, tossed the phone over the side of the patio, and buggered up my ankle.” Perhaps it was from the painfully embarrassing memories, but my ankle began to throb. “It aches when the weather changes, or if I walk on uneven ground for a long time—or talk about it.”

“Did the tomato make it?” she asked seriously, scribbling a few notes down.

“Nope, but it was a lost cause to begin with. My plants always die.” It was true, I’d yet to own a plant I was able to nurture and get to flourish.

Continuing to write, she said. “That’s probably because you’re a reaper?”

“Seriously?”

She looked up. “Most reapers have a tough time with plants and small animals, like fish.”

“Wow, I always thought I’d inherited my mother’s anti-green thumb.” We never had plants when I was growing up. When I got my own place I’d been determined to get a little green in my life. Alaskan winter days were dark and plants seemed like the perfect touch of life during the cold months. But no matter what I tried, I couldn’t get the darn things to grow. Now I knew why. “Remind me not to clean my boys’ fish tank.”

"I'll make a note here to start you on physical therapy. I can help you strengthen your ankle."

"A physical therapist too?" I liked Dr. Jensen. She didn't just listen to what I said, but seemed genuinely interested in helping me.

"I started my medical career as an assistant to a physical therapist." She smiled. "It made me want to become a doctor."

"Where would we do my physical rehab, here?" Lord knew I could use it on more than just my ankle.

"Yes. One of the benefits of working at GRS is deep pockets. I've got better equipment and supplies than most hospitals in Alaska." Her gaze tracked down the form. "Do you smoke?"

"No."

She made a checkmark. "Do you drink alcohol?'

"Yes."

"How often?"

I hated these questions. They always made me feel like I'd done something wrong. "Two to three times a week?"

She scribbled another note. "Hard liquor? Wine? Beer?

"Yes." Realizing that sounded rather alcoholicish, I added, "But I prefer beer."

Another smile spread across her face. “A girl after my own heart.”

The woman had sophistication coming out her ears and I had a difficult time picturing her downing a cold one. “I pegged you as a wine drinker?”

“One of my claims to fame in college was being the two time beer drinking champion at my sorority’s Oktoberfest.”

“Impressive.” The connection between Dr. Jensen and I tightened a little more. “But only two years?”

She flipped around a picture frame that had been facing away from me and pointed to a Muffy-looking blond. “Belinda Mayer stole the title my senior year.”

The good doc stood out amongst the sea of Barbies. “She looks really—perky.”

“Don’t let her looks fool you. The girl could drink like a fish.” She set the picture back in its place and returned her attention to the questions. “Do you use any recreational drugs?”

“Define recreational?” When she looked up with her eyebrow lifted, I rethought my answer. “No, besides the occasional swig of cold medicine to help me sleep, I’m clean.”

“Do you have trouble sleeping?”

“For the first six months after Jeff died I did, but I’m

getting better." I still woke some nights thinking he was beside me, but it didn't cause me the jolt of depression anymore. Usually, I just rolled over and fell back asleep. "No need for a prescription if that's what you're asking."

"It was." She ticked off another box. "Are you taking anything for depression?"

"Despite the opinion of others, no."

"Tomorrow you'll be given your psych exam, which includes a little chat with GRS's psychiatrist. He's good, but a little pill happy if you know what I mean." She set down her pen and looked at me. "My suggestion is to take the prescription if he writes one, and toss it when you get home. It's better to look cooperative than having to defend your mental competence."

"GRS has a psychiatrist on staff?" I shifted in my chair. "That makes me a little nervous."

"Let's face it, this isn't your ordinary nine-to-five. He's a great therapist and you might find yourself needing to talk about something that happens on the job."

I widened my eyes. "Can't I just come and see you?"

She gave a little snort. "Psychiatry is not on my list of specialties, but I will admit, I give my best advice after a few beers."

"Me too. I'm a veritable font of wisdom after a six pack."

There had been several times over the last year when Vella and I had solved the world's problems. With each bottle we became more brilliant. But, as with reality, by the morning my genius had been replace by self-loathing and a monster headache.

She scooted her chair forward and pulled a blood pressure cuff off a hook on the wall. "You'll need to take off your jacket."

Obviously there was no way I was getting out of revealing my sweatshirt. This was a good lesson for me. I'd dressed like a frump for so long, I'd become immune to it. Already this job was forcing me to give myself higher standards. I slipped off the jacket and pushed up my sleeve, resting my arm on the chair. Candace didn't comment on my poor clothing choice, and I didn't bring it to her attention.

After positioning the cuff, she pushed a button. The whir of the machine kicked in. The band tightened. I attempted a few calming breaths, trying to make my blood pressure as low as possible. The pressure reached that painful point when my hand felt three times its normal size.

A second later a tiny puff of air hissed, releasing pressure every few seconds. I mentally tried to slow my heart rate. Not having any real medical training besides what I learned from television, I didn't know if that had anything to do with my blood pressure, but figured it was worth a try. A quiet ticking clicked from the machine. The painful throbbing ebbed to a tolerable level. After another few seconds, the cuff gave a loud sigh and deflated.

"One twenty over eighty." She yanked on the strap, and with a loud rasp of Velcro, freed my arm. "Perfect."

Relief, and I'll admit, a little surprise washed through me. "Great."

She hung the cuff back up and stood. "Now, your weight."

I groaned. "Do we have too?"

"Sorry." She indicated a fancy scale the size of my treadmill. "It's required."

"That thing looks big enough to weigh livestock." She laughed as I plodded to the scale, my shoulders slumping. Before climbing on I kicked off my shoes. Like I said, any edge I could give myself. I doubted it would matter when it came to finding out just how fluffy I'd become.

I stepped on it and stared at the digital reading. The numbers scrolled quickly upward and landed on a nice round one hundred and fifty. "Holy crap."

Candace wrote the weight on the file. "It's natural to put on weight during a time of grieving, but you're young and the weight shouldn't be too difficult to take off."

She sat back at the desk and I dropped into the plum chair. "I didn't realize I gained thirty pounds."

Instead of making me feel better, her consoling smile drove home just how much I'd played into the grieving widow. Though perhaps not consciously, I'd used putting my kids' needs before mine a few times too often.

"I guarantee you'll drop some weight once you start your training." She closed the file. "Until then, try to eat better. I recommend cutting out sugar, which includes limiting your drinking."

"This job just keeps getting better and better." I let out a sigh.

"Well, we're done except for—" She opened her drawer and pulled out a plastic cup with a blue lid. "Getting a sample."

I wrinkled my nose. "There's no way I'm pregnant."

"Drug testing."

"Oh—right." I took the cup. "Bathroom?"

"Straight across the hall."

I exited the office. The bathroom mirrored the other room, with elegant granite countertops and tiled floors. I really needed to give my house a makeover. The 1970's harvest gold bathtub and black laminate counters hadn't been changed since the day the previous owners installed them.I mentally added yet another project to my growing list.

After doing my business, I handed Dr. Jensen the cup. A low growl rumbled from my stomach. I hoped we were finished. I got cranky if I went too long between meals. And after facing the harsh reality of my weight, I was definitely feeling a little grouchy. “Anything else?”

“All finished.” She walked me to the outer office. “I’ll set up a time to examine and test your ankle. From there I can set up a rehab program. In the meantime, I suggest taping it.” She reached behind the desk and pulled out a promotional pamphlet. “You can get this at most sporting goods stores, and there’s a website that shows you how to properly tape up a weak ankle.”

“Roger that, doc.” I took the brochure and my stomach grumbled again.

At that moment Nate opened the door. I had to wonder if he’d been listening outside. “Finished?”

“Yep.” I turned back to Candace. “Thanks again.”

“You’re welcome. I’ll call you later this week for rehab,” she said.

“Everything okay?” Nate sounded a little too hopeful, reminding me again that he thought I wouldn’t make a good reaper.

“Just fine.” I brushed past him. “I’m starved.”

Not waiting for him, I headed down the hall, not exactly sure how to find my way out of GRS’s inner sanctum. I can be stubborn, and my determination to prove him wrong took hold. I’d show Nate Cramer that I had what it took to be a damn fine reaper—right after I refueled with a jumbo basket of parmesan-garlic fries.

CHAPTER SEVEN

Nate offered to buy me lunch, and we ended up across the street at a restaurant I didn't particularly love. Despite Dr. Jensen's suggestion to eat better, I'm pretty picky about my food, and craved something cheesy and unhealthy. But Nate was adamant, even after I recommended a nearby diner that made the best burgers in town. *Control freak.*

I perused the menu. Greens, grains, and things I couldn't pronounce dominated the list. I ordered a Santa Fe chicken salad with extra ranch and a Diet Coke. At least I recognized the ingredients. Nate ordered the Asian chicken salad without the mandarin oranges. What's the point?

I toyed with my wrapped set of silverware "So, what's up with you and Willow? You guys have a nasty breakup or something?"

"There's nothing between me and Willow." He tapped his finger impatiently on the table.

Oh, there was definitely something between the two co-workers. "Huh." I slowly peeled the wrapper from the napkin. My innate curiosity wouldn't let the subject drop. "It sure looked like there was some history?" He didn't reply. I glanced up, but he was staring at a spot behind me. The joke was on him. I was immune to the silent treatment. I had a teenager. "Why do you hate her?"

His eyes drifted back to me. "I don't trust her."

"Because she's a beautiful, independent woman?" Nate didn't strike me as the type to be threatened by a successful woman. And I didn't know if his opinion about me not making a good reaper was personal, or a blanket judgment about women.

"The reason I don't trust her is none of your business." He glanced behind me again, narrowing his gaze. "But I suggest you keep your distance from her. She's bad news."

"Right." Sure sounded like sour grapes to me. When he didn't meet my eyes, I followed his gaze. "What are you looking at?"

"Nothing."

I craned my neck and noticed two men sitting at a table across the restaurant. They appeared normal—really normal. As a matter of fact, if Nate hadn't clued me in, I wouldn't have noticed them at all. "Do you know those two?"

"In a sense." His eyes shifted to me. "They're our competitors."

"Reapers have competitors?" Chancing another look, I assessed them. Both men appeared benign. One caught my eye and lifted his drink in silent acknowledgment. I smiled and turned back to Nate. "What kind of competitors?"

"Angels."

My mouth dropped open. "Are you serious?"

"Unfortunately, yes."

I've had a major thing for angels all my life. As a child, they were grouped in the same category as mermaids and the little people I was certain lived in my walls. After Jeff's death I took comfort in imagining them spiriting him away on heavenly wings. "That is so cool."

Nate snorted, which I took as an insult to my intelligence. "They are not cool. They're a pain in the a—"

"Hey." I cut him off before a bolt of lightning struck us for blasphemy. "If you're going to insult the heavenly hosts, do it when I'm not around."

"Trust me, they give as good as they get."

Trying to reconcile angels to the same level as us reapers went against all the beliefs I'd been raised with. Or at least the ones I'd glamorized. "I'm sure you're wrong. Angels are all loving."

"You newbies are so naïve." He sat forward and lowered his voice. I leaned away from him, fairly certain he was about to burst my bubble. "Not all angels are jerks, but those two are. They're guardian angels."

I turned and looked at the men again. Both were staring at me and smiling. Did they have x-ray hearing or some kind of all-knowingness?

"God, would you stop doing that?"

I faced Nate again. "Sorry, but this is all new to me." I took a deep breath and exhaled. "Go on."

"Guardian angels interfere with our reaping. Their job is to save their charges."

Relief washed through me. "Wow, that's so amazing and awesome."

"No." His head shook vigorously. "Not amazing, Lisa. People are meant to die at certain times. These guys come in with their free pass from Heaven and muck it up."

"Free pass?" In addition to all the paperwork and exams GRS made a new reaper go through, they obviously needed to incorporate an Afterlife 101 class. I made a mental note to bring that up to management.

"It's all part of the Free Will Project, which is stupid, in my opinion."

I glanced at the ceiling, waiting for that bolt of lightning. "Easy with the insults."

"People are going to die. Sometimes I have to attempt a reap three or four times before I get the soul."

"Wow, militant much?" I leaned forward, giving Nate my best mom face. "Souls aren't a prize you collect to reach a quota. This is somebody's life we're talking about."

"You're going to lecture me on what a soul is?"

He had a point. I really didn't know what I was talking about. I'd only officially been a reaper for a few hours. "Fine, then why are they here? Just having lunch? Are they human like us?"

"No, but they take human form when they need to." He flicked his head toward a table to my right. "See the large man at the end?"

"Yeah."

"He's about to—"

Before Nate finished his sentence, chaos erupted at the table. The big guy clutched his throat, his face turning red. I jumped to my feet. "He's choking."

The other people at the table leapt up. Chairs scooted across the tile, a few banging when they hit the floor in the panicked rush to help their friend. The two guardian angels and I started toward the table, but Nate gripped my arm. "Wait."

I yanked my arm free. "He needs the Heimlich."

"It won't matter."

My feet froze, unable to take another step. "Will the angels help him?"

"They'll try—but it won't work."

"Why not?"

"William has been slated for a long time." Nate stepped around me but didn't go any further. "Heart attack, diabetes, the man has been on borrowed time thanks to the guardians." A look of satisfaction stretched across his mouth. "I'll throw the boys a bone and let them give it their best try."

"You sound pretty confident."

"Yeah." He shrugged. "I am."

I blew out a long breath. "So that man is going to die? No matter what?"

Nate gave a single nod, continuing to smile.

It didn't matter how many years I'd reaped, I'd never become as callus as him. Just knowing there was nothing I could do for William, made my stomach turn.

The big guy's face darkened to purple. He collapsed to the floor, hands still at his throat. It was awful to watch. The wait staff and diners crowded around him, turning William on his side and pummeling his back, trying to dislodge whatever was stuck in his throat.

"Call 911," Nate said before striding toward the crowd.

It took a few seconds for his order to sink in. "Right, 911." I dug in my coat pocket and hauled out my phone. My hands shook and I kept tapping the wrong number. "Frickin' hell!" Finally I got the number dialed, and in a quivering voice, gave dispatch all the info. He assured me the ambulance was on the way and that somebody had already called. I clicked off and backed up until my legs hit the chair. I dropped heavily into it. "Holy crap."

Nate wound his way through the crowd and knelt beside the man. I saw the bottoms of his hiking boots peeking through the throng of legs. The breath froze in my chest when he stood and wove his way out of the mob with the fat guy's spirit firmly in hand.

He stopped at the table. "I need to take care of this."

"What's going on?" William's spirit looked from me to Nate. "Do I know you?"

No doubt the guy was confused—and rightly so. I knew what was going on and it was almost too much to take in. "I'm Lisa." Realizing my introduction did nothing to clarify the situation, I added. "There's been a little accident."

A woman's cry emanated from somewhere in the middle of the crowd, and the man turned toward the table he'd been sitting at. "What's going on?"

I wasn't sure how to answer him. "Well, William." I glanced at Nate, widening my eyes with a silent *jump in anytime.* "Somebody in your lunch party choked to death."

"Oh no." He spun, trying to get a better look. "Was it Charlie? It had to be Charlie. The man shovels food in like a conveyor belt."

"No." I shook my head. "Charlie is fine."

"It's you, William." Nate could really use a lesson in tactfulness. "You're dead."

William glanced from Nate to me, and then started laughing, the white aura round his translucent form growing. "How can I be dead when I'm standing here talking to you?"

"Yeah, that's a tricky one." My gaze leveled on Nate. He seemed impatient to get the job done. Maybe this was some kind of on-the-job training. I pinned him with my best glare before turning back to William. I let my ire morph into the same type of smile I used when comforting my kids. "Nate will be escorting you to your final destination." The explanation made me sound like a paranormal travel agent. "There's nothing to be afraid of. I can tell your journey is going to be very enjoyable." By the bright white of his aura I assumed he'd be going to Heaven. Hopefully I wasn't making a rookie mistake. My smile widened. "If you just go with Nate, he'll get you on your way."

William didn't move. "I'd like to see for myself."

I assumed William meant he wanted to see his body. Unsure if this followed procedure; I looked at Nate for confirmation. He nodded. Not letting go of the big man's spirit, they edged toward the crowd. A lump grew inside of my throat and my nose tingled. I'm usually not a crier, but the forlorn look on William's face pushed all my buttons. He seemed so lost. After a few seconds, his wide shoulders slumped. From what I noticed Nate did nothing to comfort him. No arm around his shoulder. No pat on the back.

Mental note to self: Be interactive with clients.

Another minute passed before they headed back to where I waited. I took a deep breath and smiled again, certain this time I looked more sad than encouraging. "Are you okay?" That was probably a really stupid question, but nothing more profound came to mind.

He shrugged. "Yeah, I think I am. I mean, it's not every day a man witnesses his own death, right?"

Heck if I knew. Maybe they did. This whole afterlife thing was almost as new to me as it was William. But I knew he didn't need my uncertainty. "Just think, you now have the answer to one of the great mysteries. There really is life after death."

That made him smile. "I guess you're right." He turned to Nate, who still held onto William's shoulder, but with only one hand. Rambo Reaper must have surmised William wasn't a flight risk. "I'm ready."

"Come with me." Nate took a step to the side, but

didn't let go. "We'll need a little privacy for this."

In a busy restaurant there was really only one place that was private. "The bathroom again?" Nate ignored me and guided William forward. Feeling like I should say something, I quietly called, "Safe journey."

The big man gave me a little wave and then turned the corner, leaving me standing alone. How long would the reaping process take? The memory of my own experience in the Holiday bathroom was convoluted. To me it felt like hours. In reality it had probably only been a few minutes and that included Nate's pitch to become a reaper.

I sat on the wooden chair and waited. The faint wail of sirens grew, but this time the sound didn't make me nervous. Ever since my husband died, the screech would send a wave of anxiety through me. I always wondered if somebody was hurt or dead. Morbid I know, but I couldn't help it. At least this time I knew. In an odd way that knowledge gave me a little comfort.

The waitress stopped at the table and set a Diet Coke next to me. "Can you believe this?"

That was a loaded question. I shook my head. "No." I picked up my soda and took a long drink.

"Second one this year. Weird."

"Yeah." It wasn't the most intelligent response, but she really didn't seem to be talking with me as much as *at* me.

She continued to stare at the crowd. “Your salads will be out in a minute.” Then she walked away, leaving me to my thoughts.

My appetite evaporated, which was a miracle in itself. I leaned back in the chair and crossed my arms. The notion that life went on even after one departed this Earth made me contemplative. William was dead but in a few minutes I’d be served the salad I’d ordered before he’d hitched a ride on the express train to Heaven. It made life’s problems seem a little less urgent.

I glanced back at the table and noticed the two guardian angels. They both stared at me, no longer smiling, but not really angry. Unsure what to do I lifted my glass. “Better luck next time guys.”

They tipped their heads toward me and turned to leave. I’m not sure what I expected. Maybe for them to wink out in a sparkle of white light. I took a sip of soda. This death gig was nothing like I’d imagined it would be.

Nate returned and slid into the chair across from me. He picked up his water and drank. I watched him. There was an edge to him even though he looked composed.

“You all right?” I had to ask. It was in my nature.

His gaze followed the EMTs wheeling a gurney toward William’s body. “I’m always all right.”

I highly doubted that. Nobody is *always* all right. At the best of times I'm sixty-five percent all right. "Okay, just asking."

The salads arrived and we each picked at the field of greens. It seemed wrong to eat while the crew worked on William—even though we knew he was in a better place. The fork stopped halfway to my mouth. "He went to Heaven, right?"

Nate nodded, pushing a small slice of orange that had snuck in on his salad to the side of his plate.

More questions popped into my head. "What kind of souls do you reap?"

He slowly chewed, his gaze leveled on me. After he swallowed, he said, "Violent deaths."

Yikes, no wonder he was so distant. Facing that much ugliness all the time would darken anybody's day. "Did Jeff reap violent deaths?"

"No." He took another large bite of salad, waiting to answer until he swallowed again. "His were more…random—deaths that didn't fall so neatly into a category."

I wasn't sure I understood completely. "Do choking victims have their own reapers?" I slid a generous pile of salad into my mouth.

He glanced down at his plate. "That reap would have

been yours, but since you haven't been trained, I took it."

A black bean lodged in my throat and I choked. Coughs seized me. I hacked and wheezed—very unladylike. Finally I was able to suck in a big gulp of air. "You knew William was going to die?"

"Yeah, I got word when you were having your medical exam." He shoveled a chunk of chicken and lettuce into his mouth.

Water, I needed water. The reaper business had just gotten real. It was one thing to be guided through the process and quite another to know I'd be responsible for getting a soul to its appropriate destination. I grabbed Nate's glass and took a big gulp. He continued to chew and stare at me. "So just what kind of deaths do I reap? Accidental deaths?"

Looking at his plate again, he jabbed at his salad. "Not exactly."

When he didn't expound on his explanation, I rapped my knuckles on the table. "What's my assignment, Nate?" From the way he avoided my eyes I knew I wasn't going to like it. At that moment my agreement to be a reaper for the sake of a paycheck seemed a tad impulsive. "I'm not responsible for plague or something gross, am I?"

"No." He set down his fork. "You'll be reaping people who died in a less than intelligent manner."

I processed what he was saying. "You mean, I'll be

reaping stupid people?"

"The people aren't stupid, just the way they die."

Still not sure I completely understood—hoping that what I thought wasn't what he meant—I pressed on. "You mean like frat boys who jump into a shallow pool or a drunk who lights his farts and burns to death?"

"Yeah, kind of like that."

The urge to laugh rivaled with my inability to speak. It just frickin' figured my assignment would be peppered with the idiotic. I sat back in my chair and stared at the dispersing crowd. The EMTs wheeled William out and things were calming. "Why William?"

Nate wrinkled his forehead. "Why William what?"

"Why would I have reaped William? He choked, that's accidental, not really stupid."

"Choking falls under you because it's kind of a miscellaneous death. It's not really violent and it's not suicide."

"Miscellaneous, that seems a little vague to me." If what Nate said was true, I was going to be a busy reaper. "What other…" I made air quotes on either side of my head. "Miscellaneous deaths fall under my watch?"

He rattled off an impressive and oppressive list. "Slipping and falling. This includes public places, homes, and mountain tops." Before I squeaked out a colorful curse about how the hell I was supposed to reap somebody lying on a ledge eight thousand feet up, he cut me off. "Most electrocutions, alcohol poisoning, sex acts gone wrong." He paused. "If they were mutual and not a homicide. Otherwise those fall under me."

My mouth hung open and for a few seconds I couldn't form an intelligent response. "So, basically any asinine way somebody could die—I get."

Cocking his head, he crossed his arms over his chest. "That's not going to be a problem is it?"

I snapped my mouth shut. "Problem? Why would reaping the recipients of the Darwin Award be a problem?" My voice raised an octave. "Who wouldn't love reaping the butt of life's jokes?"

"Jeff never had a problem with it."

I narrowed my gaze. "Let's get one thing straight. I am not Jeff."

A purely insulting laugh huffed from Nate. "Oh, I'm well aware of that."

Damn, I'd walked right into that one. Ever since I'd fallen into this reaper gig, Nate had made it quite clear he didn't think I was up to the task. Determination coursed through me. That happened sometimes—I'd get angry and dig in my heels. Usually I got far more than I bargained for.

That happened with Bronte's fifth grade science

project. What started out with good intentions, ended with a lot of tears and a thirty-pound, pudding-spewing volcano. Not only did I have to transport the monstrosity, I had to clean up its stunning eruption at the show, which covered the table, floor, and several surrounding science projects.

Before I repeated the mistake by making promises I might not be able to keep, I slid from the chair. "I've lost my appetite." I scooped up my purse and slung it over my shoulder. "I assume you got the check?"

When he didn't reply, I walked out of the restaurant. I'd like to say I felt some satisfaction about snubbing him, but the only thing I felt was humiliated. I reaped stupid people. Great. Like I didn't get enough of them in my personal life.

CHAPTER EIGHT

The kids tumbled through the front door an hour after I got home from lunch with Nate. Pasting on an *everything's wonderful* face, I met them at the entrance to the kitchen. "How was your day?"

Bronte slinked past me, earbuds in place. "Lame, like always."

Breck dropped his backpack at the door and made a beeline for the refrigerator. "Hi, Mom."

Bryce, always more composed, hung his coat on the hook, and then followed his brother to find refreshments. "It was good. A guy came to our class and dissected a cow eye."

"Yeah." Breck shoved a cheese stick in his mouth. "I poked my finger in the victorious layer."

"Vitreous layer," Bryce corrected.

"Whatever, it was so cool when it squished out."

I grabbed the back of Breck's collar. "Take off your jacket and stay a while."

He shrugged out of it, switching the cheese to his other hand and extracting his arm. "Come on, Bryce, Tiffany Powers and the Techno Werewolves is on."

"No TV." I pointed to their backpacks. "Homework."

A unanimous groan circled the kitchen. Bronte shoved Bryce out of her way and pulled a bottle of flavored water out of the fridge. "I'm all done."

I lifted an eyebrow. Over the last year I'd let the kids skate when it came to homework and extra chores. The teachers had done the same thing because of Jeff's death. I'd convinced myself it was for their own good, at least until they could adjust. But lunch with Nate had changed things. He didn't think I'd make a good reaper. Whether I would or not I'd be damn if I'd curl up in a ball and prove him right.

With a sense of empowerment, and no small dose of *I'll show you,* I made the decision it was time for the entire Carron family to get their crap together. "Good. Let me see it."

Bronte stared at me, slowly twisting the cap off the bottle. I knew this look. She was sizing me up. Probably trying to figure out if I was serious. Then she attempted a diversion tactic. "I left it at school."

"Huh." I gripped the edge of the refrigerator door and

closed it. “Okay, then help me make dinner.”

Her eyebrows pinched together and the corner of her lip lifted in a tiny sneer. “I don’t do cooking?”

“You live here too. We all need to pitch in.” I bent and opened the door to the dishwasher. “You can start by unloading the dishes.”

With an incensed huff, she trudged the three feet to the dishwasher. “This is a complete waste of my talent, Mother.”

“Mine too.” I held out a clean plate to her. “If you don’t want to help with dinner, clean your room or…show me your homework.”

She took the plate from me. “What’s with the whole *mom* gig? You haven’t made us do chores for the last year.”

“It’s time we get back into a routine.” I paused, not knowing how she’d feel about me going back to work. “And…good news… I got a job. I start full-time next week.”

“What kind of job?” She turned and stared at me, her tone suggesting I wasn’t qualified for much beyond scrubbing toilets.

I pulled another plate from the lower rack. “Actually, I got a job at GRS.”

“Like Dad?”

“Same company, different job.”

Her gaze narrowed. “Doing what?”

On the way home I'd thought about what I'd tell the kids. It had to be something believable but also gave me an excuse for travel or inconvenient hours. "Human resource assistant. I'll be helping employees with employment issues." I set the plate on the counter. "I might even get to do a little village travel." To my trained ear I sounded like I was trying too hard to convince her, so eased back on the enthusiasm. "GRS has employees all over the state."

"I find that utterly fascinating." Clearly she didn't.

"What you should find fascinating is the money. We might even be able to have a descent Christmas."

Her eyes lit up. "Like—a new laptop—merry?"

I shrugged. "Maybe, if you pull your grades up, plus help around the house."

She slid the second dish onto the shelf, continuing to stare at me. I waited. My daughter was sharp and calculating. Either she was devising a counter attack to keep her freedom or she was surmising the situation. Another few seconds passed. Then, to my surprise, she nodded. "Okay."

She turned and walked toward the door. "Where are you going?"

"To do my homework."

With that, she left. The sound of her backpack unzipping whispered through the kitchen doorway. I couldn't help but smile. It was a small victory, but one I would happily take. Having Bronte working *with* me and not *against* me would make my life a heck of a lot easier.

The sound of a car door thumping closed was followed by clomping footsteps and then our front door opening. “Hello, hello.”

“I’m in the kitchen, Vella.” I continued to unload the dishwasher.

Such a good friend. She entered bearing a six pack and a bag of groceries. “You haven’t started dinner yet, have you?”

She knew me so well. “Not yet.”

“Bud is out of town this week and I got a little carried away with my grocery shopping.” She set the plastic bag on the table. “So I thought why not dine with my favorite people. We could fix the kids dinner, set them in front of the TV, and have us a few icy ones.” Her voice dropped to a whisper. “And you can tell me about your day.”

When Vella had that look, I knew I was in for eighty questions. “The kids should love that.”

“I figure that will keep them occupied while we chat.” She dug in the bag and pulled out a roasted chicken, a tub of mashed potatoes, gravy, and a tin of biscuits. “Pop these in the oven.” She handed me the tube. “They only take eight minutes.”

“Do some shopping today?” I asked, peeling the

wrapper from the biscuit container.

"I worked a little this morning, but when my two o'clock color canceled, I decided that retail therapy was a better use of my time." She arranged the containers on the table. "I'd planned on buying a new pair of boots, but then remembered I didn't have any food in the house."

Vella not having any food in the house meant she was out of wine. "No splurging on footwear then?"

"Girl, Bud's been riding my butt about staying on budget. He's as tight as my Aunt Edith's girdle when it comes to money." She dragged out the chair and sat. "But I like my comforts and he knew that before he married me."

"That's right. Having a trophy wife comes at a price," I said over my shoulder.

Bud was a decade older than Vella. I don't think he knew just how high maintenance a southern trophy wife could be. But to be fair, Vella loved Bud and treated him like gold. "It's nice that you're trying to stay within budget. That should make him happy."

"I know, right? Tight old miser." She waved a manicured hand in the air. "I never let him grocery shop anymore. The last time he bought the cheapest toilet paper in the store. I swear he actually dug around in their storeroom to find the last existing package."

"And that was a bad thing?"

"You have no idea. I couldn't tell if it was toilet paper or sand paper. I'm delicate down there."

A snicker slipped out. "Ouch."

Vella jabbed a finger at me. "I kid you not. I could have rubbed myself with tree bark and gotten the same results."

I grimaced at the thought.

"Anyway," she continued, "today I bought me some of that really expensive toilet paper. The kind with three layers that looks like my grandma quilted it." She gave a little sigh. "It's like wiping my ass with a baby angel."

The vivid image Vella wove made me burst out laughing

"Seriously!" Her eyes widened and her expression turned serious. "I'll give you some and you be the judge."

I smacked the tube of biscuits on the edge of the counter. Thick white dough oozed between the cardboard. Why was it I loved everything devoid of nutrition? After laying the fat circles on a cookie sheet, I popped them into the oven. "I've obviously lived a deprived life."

"You joke, but it's true." Vella glanced over her shoulder and then back at me, lowering her voice. "So?"

"So what?"

She gave me her frowny face. "You know what. GRS."

I held up a finger and walked to the kitchen door. No kids in sight. I hoped they were actually doing their homework, but figured I could follow up on that later. Baby steps. “We are definitely going to need alcohol for this.” I found a bottle opener and popped the caps off two beers. “Where do I begin?”

“First of all, did you go this morning?” Vella plucked two glasses from the cabinet. “Was *he* there?”

By *he,* I assumed she meant Nate. “Oh yes, *he* was there.” While pouring the first glass, I took a deep breath. “And so were about fifty GRS workers.” I tossed the bottle into the trash and handed her the glass. “The grim kind, if you know what I mean.”

Her mouth dropped open and her eyes rounded. “Get out of here.”

I nodded. “Yep, seems he was telling the truth and I am—” My voice dropped to a whisper. “A grim reaper.”

Vella picked up a glass and took a long drink. After which, she wiped her mouth with the sleeve of her shirt. Though it wasn’t uncommon for her white trash roots to come out, it was always funny to witness. She opened her mouth to say something, stopped, and then took another gulp. I waited. I knew how she felt. Finding out her best friend was an angel of death was a lot to take in.

She swallowed hard and set the glass on the counter.

"Well, if that isn't the shit."

"If you mean messed up, then yeah, that's the shit." After snagging the full glass, I sat at the table. "But it's a paying job and there are benefits."

"That's good—right?"

Obviously she was struggling for the right thing to say. Vella joined me at the table. On impulse, she reached across the table to pat my arm, but stopped. We both stared at her hovering hand.

"It's all right," I said, "you can touch me."

Tension eased from her shoulders and she lowered her hand, tapping my arm once as if she thought it would explode.

I smirked. "Any bright lights you feel drawn to?"

"No." She pulled back her hand. "But you can never be too careful. I don't know what a reaper does and doesn't do." Vella ran her finger around the rim of the glass. "And you're sure about this? He wasn't just putting you on?"

"It would have been an elaborate jest." I lowered my voice so the kids wouldn't overhear, and recounted my day. Vella sat riveted in her chair. Even though the story sounded outlandish, something I would conjure after huffing airplane glue, I'd finally accepted it was true.

When I finished, Vella sat for a few seconds, staring at me. Then she smiled. The action was forced and a little tight, devoid of her genuine southern cheer. “You seem okay with all this.”

I shrugged. “What choice do I have? I need a job. The pay and benefits are better than anything I could get elsewhere.”

“I guess.”

“What’s wrong?” I knew my friend and usually there were five or six interactive conversations happening in her head at once. “You sound…wary.”

“It’s not that. I’m just so angry with Jeff. Why didn’t he ever tell you about this?”

I tried to smile but it felt more like a grimace. “They said we’re not supposed to reveal ourselves to anybody. Not even family members.”

“But you just told me.” A panicked note elevated Vella’s voice an octave.

“Yeah, but you already knew about the Holiday station and Nate.” My explanation wasn’t quelling her alarm. “Don’t worry. Nothing is going to happen to you. I’m sure of it.”

“If it does, I’m coming back to haunt you.” She took a big gulp of beer. “And I’ll be damned if I’m going to the light easily.”

“Thanks for the warning.” I hadn’t thought what it would be like to reap somebody I knew. Knowing my pool of friends and family, it would no doubt happen one day. "But I'm sure it's going to be fine." She glared at me. "Really, I promise."

"I'm going to hold you to that." Vella took a deep breath and exhaled. "How dangerous is this reaper job anyway?"

"I don't know. The people are already dead. How dangerous can it be?" I paused. Something about Jeff's death nagged at me. "But…"

"But what?"

"I can't help but wonder if Jeff's car accident wasn't an accident."

"Why do you say that?" Leaning in, Vella rested her elbows on the table. "Did somebody say something today?"

I tried to ignore the shiver of foreboding rippling through me. "Not in so many words but I kept getting the feeling there was more to it than a simple car crash." I shrugged. "I'm probably imagining it. Trying to reconcile him being a reaper and not telling me is probably making me suspicious."

"I know you guys had your problems, every couple does, but Jeff was a good guy."

"Yeah, he was." I nodded. "Maybe I'm feeling guilty about thinking he cheated on me." The oven timer beeped, pulling me away from my remorseful thoughts.

After silencing the piercing buzzer, I slipped on and oven mitt and removed the golden brown biscuits and set them on the stove. “Once I get a little more familiar with GRS I think I might ask around. Surely somebody will be able to reassure me.”

Vella started loading up plates for the kids. “What about Nate?”

“He’s as closed mouth as a mafia hit man.” I plopped a biscuit onto each plate. “But there’s a woman named Willow in payroll. Maybe she knows something.”

“It’s worth a try.”

Despite Vella’s encouraging words, she didn’t seem optimistic. Maybe she was worried I’d learn something I didn’t want to know. What’s that saying? Don’t ask the question if you don’t want the answer. “Kids, time to eat.”

The thunder of at least four feet pounded through the house. Bryce and Breck slid into their chairs at the table as if stealing second base. I always waited to set their drinks down until they’d settled. Too much spilled milk over the years. Bronte wandered in still connected to Apple support. I pointed to my ears. Getting my message, she yanked on the cord and shoved the headphones into her pocket. I assumed her music continued to play but didn’t point that out to her. I take my wins where I can.

Yummy noises emanated from the table. It wasn’t the

healthiest meal in the world but all three ate. Score. Vella and I dished up plates for ourselves, making sure to take all we wanted in the first helping. When the food was good, we usually didn't get a chance for seconds. Like a swarm of locusts, the kids polished off everything but the chicken bones.

I looked at Vella and smiled. "That has to be a new record."

She laughed. "Maybe I should have bought more."

The boys scooted from their chairs and started out the door.

"Bus your dishes." They stopped, appearing confused. It was the first time I'd asked them to do anything in the last year. Obviously, further instructions were needed. "Pick up your plate, scrape it in the garbage, and put it in the dishwasher."

Simple and to the point. That's what worked best with eight-year-old boys. Besides Bryce needing to do a double scrape to get the mashed potato residue off, the boys did a great job. Not having to be told, Bronte followed suit.

Kids fed in eight point three minutes.

After closing the dishwasher, she leaned in and gave me a kiss on the cheek, and then walked out. I glanced at Vella. She was as surprised as I was at my elusive daughter's display of affection, and dare I hoped—approval.

“What was that all about?”

The faintest tingle burned behind my eyes. I inhaled, not wanting to have a gushy mom moment. “I told her I got a job and made her do her homework.”

Vella nodded. “Boundaries. Kids think they don’t want them, but they do.”

“Come on, let’s sit.” I brushed the biscuit crumbs to the center of the table before claiming Breck’s vacated chair. “Thanks for dinner.” I held up my glass. “And the beer.”

“You don’t have to thank me. I need girl time just as much as you do.” She sat in the spot Bronte had vacated. “So what’s going on tomorrow?”

I groaned. “Psychological testing.”

Vella cocked her head to the side. “What, to see if you’re nuts?”

“Ironic, isn’t it?”

“I’d say. Who wouldn’t be a little off kilter after everything you’ve been through?” Her eyebrows arched. “What kind of testing do they do?”

“An oral exam, I think.”

“Normally I’d look forward to something like that, but I don’t think it’s going to be as good as it sounds.”

It had been a long time since I’d had anything *oral* given to me. Unfortunately I had to agree with Vella. “Me either, but I’ll give you details if it is.”

"Girl, I want details even if it's not."

I shoved a forkful of mashed potatoes in my mouth and swallowed. "Not afraid of being smited for knowing too much?"

"Nah." She downed the last of her beer. "Like Mark Twain said, 'You go to Heaven for the climate, but you go to Hell for the company.' I figure I'll be so busy visiting my relatives and friends I won't have time to wallow in eternal damnation."

I laughed. "Good point."

My day started out with a lot of unknowns, and ended with even more. But a few things were certain. My best friend wouldn't abandon me, no matter how nuts things got, and I'd do just about anything to provide for my kids. Even if that meant reaping stupid people.

Jeff's death still bothered me, but those questions could wait. It wasn't like knowing exactly what happened to him would change my life more than it already had. I doubted there was some huge conspiracy or nefarious plot that landed him on the pointy end of the reapers scythe. Right?

CHAPTER NINE

Twenty minutes. The tick-tock from the cuckoo-clock marked the passage of time. Time, by my calculations, that had morphed into an endless stretch of boredom. I shifted on the chaise lounge, trying to get comfortable. Though tempted, I refused to lie down. This was the psychologist's office, and everything in me fought being analyzed. Reclining felt too much like giving into the process.

I glanced at the irritating clock again. Twenty-one minutes. The doctor, or whoever was supposed to administer this test, was late. Either he or she was being completely rude or this was part of the test. My gaze scanned the office for obvious hidden cameras. I didn't see anything, thus the hidden part, so I waited and refrained from fidgeting.

After another minute the door opened and a man entered. "Mrs. Carron?"

I stood and smiled like I hadn't been contemplating

smashing his cuckoo-clock against the floor. "Yes."

"James T. Crock. I'm so sorry I'm late." I bit the inside of my cheek, trying not to laugh at his name. He dumped a stack of files onto his desk and stuck out his hand. "Had an unscheduled meeting."

When I shook his hand his fingers were cold and clammy. The urge to wipe my palm against the fabric of my jeans was only overridden by my thoughts of conspiracy. Was my every move being scrutinized? "No problem. I was just sitting here admiring your clock."

A wide smile stretched across his mouth. "It's German. Got it when I visited the Black Forest." He glanced at the clock, and then at me again. "I find it very soothing. Don't you?"

Not so much. But I smiled and nodded, wanting to get on Dr. Crock's good side.

"Well then, shall we get started?" He pointed at two overstuffed chairs near the window. "The test is rather lengthy so we might as well get comfortable."

He gathered a leather portfolio and claimed one of the chairs. I sat in the other and crossed my legs, trying to appear at ease. Inside, my stomach flip-flopped like a spawning salmon. I attempted small talk. "James T. Crock, like James T. Kirk, huh?"

"No." He looked up from the stack of papers he'd

been thumbing through. "I was named after James T. Cook, the great explorer."

"Ah." *Okay, not a Star Trek fan.* "Great man."

"If by great you mean an actual historical figure, who was instrumental in developing ways to measure longitudinal bearings, then yes, he was quite exceptional."

"Uh yep, that's exactly what I meant." Obviously small talk was not his forte, so I decided to let Dr. Crock take the lead.

He leveled a stare at me and I found myself sitting a little straighter. "I will administer the test orally." I suppressed the urge to giggle. It didn't matter who said it, *orally* always sounded dirty. "Your reply will be either yes or no. There's no need to expound on why you've answered one way or another. Just a simple yes or no."

As far as I was concerned the sooner I finished, the sooner I could have lunch. I nodded again. "Fast and to the point, got it."

He gave me a placating smile, but I don't think he actually believed I could follow directions. I'd show him.

"Are you ready?" His pen hovered over the question sheet in his portfolio.

"Fire away."

"Question one, I like mechanics magazines."

"Excuse me?" I wasn't sure I'd heard him correctly.

“I like mechanics magazines. Yes or no.”

“No.” It was the first answer that popped into my head, mainly because I’d never read a mechanics magazine. Still, I guess if I’d had any interest in that area I would have picked up one up from the store. I answered again, very firm in my conviction that I indeed did not like mechanic magazines. “No.”

He made a little checkmark on the sheet. “Question two. My sleep is fitful and disturbed.”

Well that was a given considering everything I’d been through the last year. But until Jeff’s accident I’d slept like a baby. “Do you mean before my husband’s death or after?”

No emotion played across Dr. Crock’s face. “My sleep is fitful and disturbed.”

Okay, no help from the help. I was tempted to say no but I’d already given myself away. Damn, I had to stay one step ahead of these questions or he’d think I was a nut case. “Yes.”

“I have a good appetite.”

“Yes.” The answer blurted from my mouth before I had a chance to think about it. “I mean it’s pretty obvious, isn’t it?”

“Yes or no, Mrs. Carron.”

“Yes, definitely yes.”

He added another tick to his paper. “I believe in the afterlife.”

I stared at him for a second. “Are you serious with that question? You realize I’m a grim reaper, right?”

“I don’t write the questions, Mrs. Carron. I only administer the test.”

“Yes, Dr. Crock, I believe in an afterlife. I’ve actually seen what waits on the other side and it didn’t look all that great.” He scribbled a note on the edge of the paper. That couldn’t be good. I inhaled and mentally centered myself again. “Next question.”

“I have never been sorry that I’m a girl.”

For the love of God. “Seven days out of the month I’m sorry I’m a girl.” I crossed my arms over my chest. “Those commercials of women riding bikes and roller skating—all lies.”

“Is that a yes then?”

I held up my hand. “Not necessarily. Other than the cramping and the irrational bouts of rage, I like being a girl.”

He arched a brow. “Yes or no.”

He was trying to trick me. I knew it. “What was the question again?”

“I have never been sorry that I’m a girl.”

After mentally repeating the sentence three times I smiled. “Yes.”

Tick.

"I sometimes tease animals."

"No, well, my mom put a sweater on our bulldog once, and I made fun of him, but no, I don't tease animals. That's just mean."

He gave a heavy sigh and marked the paper. "I do not like everyone I know."

My mind raced through my list of people in my life. I didn't hate anybody, but I didn't necessarily like everybody. Take my neighbor, Clare Goucher. The woman was pushing sixty and insisted on doing yard work in her bikini. Or my mom. I loved her, but I didn't really like her most of the time. "Yes, I do not like everyone I know." Dr. Crock's mouth pinched into a tight line. "It's unrealistic to like everybody, isn't it?"

"I'm not here to judge, Mrs. Carron."

I bit back a sarcastic retort, not wanting another side note added to my file. Instead I focused on the damn clock. "Next."

"I am neither gaining weight nor losing weight."

"Another fat question, huh?" I drummed my fingers against my ribs. The tight waist of my jeans decided my answer. "No."

Tick.

Bastard. I was really starting to *not like* Dr. Crock.

“Once in a while I laugh at a dirty joke.”

“Yes.” I kept my eyes on the clock. The sooner this stupid test was over, the better.

“I sweat very easily on cool days.”

What the hell? This test seemed to be skewed toward us fluffy gals, and I didn’t like it. Most days in Alaska were cool, thankfully. “No.”

“I believe I’m being followed.”

That question gave me pause. Did ravens count? Because I was fairly certain that bird was stalking me. “Yes.”

Dr. Crock’s brows lifted in surprise. I could tell he wanted to ask whom I thought was following me, but when I narrowed my eyes at him, he cleared his throat. “Peculiar odors come to me at times.”

I blinked several times. “What?”

“Peculiar odors come to me at times.”

“Dr. Crock, I have two eight year old boys. They produce odors no human should be subjected to.”

“That would be a yes, I assume?”

“Yes.” I’m pretty sure that’s not what the question meant. I’d read accounts where people swore they smelled their dead grandmother’s perfume. Nothing like that had ever happened, so I stuck with what I knew. Besides, this test was pissing me off.

“The things that some of my family have done have frightened me.”

“Yes, yes, and yes.” There was a lifetime of therapy wrapped up in having a cop for a dad. Not to mention my brother, whom I believe was dropped on his head as a baby. Though my mom denies it. “Definitely, yes.”

“I like or have liked fishing.”

I’m an Alaskan. Fishing is in our blood. “Yes.”

Dr. Crock pinned me with a stare. “I deserve severe punishment for my sins.”

Call me crazy, but the way he looked at me made me wonder if that question was even on the test. “We all sin, but I don’t feel I need to be severely punished for them.” He continued to stare at me, giving me the willies. “Do you?”

“Again, Mrs. Carron, not judging.”

Right. “How many more questions are there?” I glanced at the clock. We’d only been at it for ten minutes.

“Five hundred total.”

I groaned and let my head fall back on the chair. “Fine. Next.”

“I like to take a bath.”

“Yes.” I said to the ceiling.

“Horses that don’t pull should be beaten or kicked.”

I started to feel like one of those horses. “No.”

“I like mannish women.”

My head popped up. "What do you mean? As in friendship or like—like?"

"You must interpret the question yourself."

"If I have to interpret the questions myself, what's the point of this test? I might say I like mannish women because I'm a lesbian, and like to feel girly. Or maybe my best friend is mannish, and I like her despite the fact that she's mannish. In each scenario the reasons are completely different."

"You're overthinking things. Just a simple yes or no."

"Then yes, I like mannish women. I like feminine women. I like feminine men if they are a good person."

He rolled his eyes as he made another checkmark on the paper. Was rolling eyes even allowed if you were a psychologist?

"I think Lincoln was greater than Washington."

Propping my elbows on the arms of the chair, I stared at Dr. Crock. Did my answers really matter? I was beginning to think it was my reaction to this barrage of idiotic questions that GRS was really gauging. "Yes."

"I have to urinate no more often than others?"

I kept my expression passive. "Yes."

On and on the questions went. Did I like to play hopscotch? Was I opposed to every person on earth drinking alcohol? Was I afraid of fire?

Three hours later Dr. Crock looked up from his paper and smiled. “Only three more questions.”

My butt cheeks throbbed from sitting so long. The entire time, he allowed me only one five-minute break to stand and stretch. I straightened my legs and sat up straight, waiting.

“I prefer to wear black clothing.”

Easy. Any woman who struggled with her weight knew black was her best friend. “Yes.”

“I’ve contemplated suicide.”

I was taken aback. Never, not even in my most grief-stricken moment, had I thought about killing myself. I had the kids. They needed me. No didn’t seem strong enough. “Never.”

He made his mark and then smiled at me. “Last question.” I saw he was just as happy to be finished with this test as I was. “I have a normal level of interest in death.”

Even though he waited for a yes or no, a lot of other answers came to my mind. “I’m a grim reaper, so already my level of interest is higher than non-reapers. So who are we gauging this by? Overall humankind or just GRS workers?” He opened his mouth to give me what I was sure would be a bland retort, but I cut him off. “On the other hand, you would think being a grim reaper would amp up my interest, but honestly, if I never ever saw another dead person, I'd be perfectly content." I stood and picked up my purse. "So you decide, Dr. Crock. Do I have a normal level of interest in death?"

I walked to the door, but stopped. When I looked back, the good doc was jotting more than a quick note in my chart. Deciding silence was golden, even though that realization had probably come too late, I walked out. The questions he'd asked had been weird, revealing, and on the rare occasion, thought provoking. I'd never contemplated whether dirt frightened me, or if my hands and feet were normally warm. Now that he'd asked, I found myself thinking about just how unenlightened I was about myself.

The reality was, I'd lost interest in the little things I once found fascinating. As a kid I spent hours watching the worms that surfaced after a rain. Now I didn't even notice them. My head was filled with to-do lists and the needs of others. Somewhere along the line I ceased being Lisa and turned into somebody's mom and wife.

In general, I thought the personality profile I'd just suffered through was crap, but I couldn't deny some of the question sparked a desire to know myself again. Did I prefer mango over guava juice? Had I ever tried guava juice? Being a grim reaper may not have been my first choice of employment, but the fact I was one of the few on Earth, gave me a shot of self-respect I hadn't felt in a long time.

Maybe I'd pick up a mechanics magazine on the way home.

CHAPTER TEN

The gymnasium spread out before me with an obstacle course that ranged from reasonable to bizarre. I assumed I was supposed to traverse this bad boy. The track I could handle. It was some of the other areas I wasn't quite sure about.

Nate stood beside me with a clipboard and a huge stopwatch. "You have ten minutes to make it through the entire course."

I nodded as if that wouldn't be a problem. "Gotcha."

"Let's walk the course first." He started down the track, not waiting for me. "You'll do one lap, then you'll veer to this area."

A pommel horse blocked our path, but luckily a springboard sat in front of it. I remember vaulting over one when I was in grade school. Of course I was seventy pounds lighter, but I think I could manage this. "I have to spring over?"

"Yes." Stepping around me, Nate moved to the next obstacle. "Here you need to climb the rope ladder."

Ladder? It was more like a spider web of knots and rope spreading across one wall. Still, not impossible. I pointed upward. "What's that?"

"Once at the top, you'll climb onto that ledge, crawl to the end, and slide down the rope."

Resting in a deep hole in the floor sat a small trampoline. The rope's end knot dangled several feet above it. Obviously, Nate expected me to drop onto the stretchy black surface. My aim would have to be good, or I'd end up sprawled on one of the mats surrounding the trampoline. At this point my biggest fear was breaking a leg or pulling muscles I hadn't used in years. "So drop onto that?"

"Drop, bounce a few times, and transfer to the next trampoline."

No problem—if I were an Olympic gymnast. The next trampoline was half the size of the other. I craned my neck to make sure there wasn't yet another, smaller apparatus I'd be expected to rebound onto. Relief washed through me when I saw a balance beam. "Got it." Boy I was being cooperative. Last night I'd decided not to whine if I could help it. "Next?"

"Climb onto the wide balance beam. Jump down." He strode ahead of me, patting each wooden beam as he passed them. "Onto the next bar." I noticed it was a bit narrower, only about three inches wide. "Down, and finally to the last balance beam."

Was he serious? The piece was no more than a half-inch across. "You expect me to walk on this?"

He stopped and at looked me. "Actually I don't think you'll make it over the vault."

Walked right into that one. I smiled. "So encouraging."

He shrugged. "You asked."

Note to self: Nate thinks you're a doofus. Don't give him ammunition.

I crossed my arms over my chest. "Fine, what's next?"

"Another lap around the track. The time will stop when you cross the finish line."

"Perfect." I screwed my determination into place. I might not vault over the horse like a gazelle, or gracefully scramble up the rope, but I sure as heck was going to finish this course in less than ten minutes. I yanked on the bottom of my sweatshirt. "Let's do this."

"Toes to the line." Nate pointed to the yellow stripe running the width of the track.

I placed one foot against the starting line and then hunkered down into a runner's stance, bouncing a couple of times like I'd seen the athletes do.

He cleared his throat. "What are you doing?"

"Getting ready to run? What does it look like?"

"You don't want me to answer that."

I twisted my head around to glare at him. "You got that right." Setting up again, I leveled my gaze on the track in front of me. "I'm ready."

"All righty, then."

I heard the laughter in his voice. *Eat my dust, Nate Cramer.*

"On your mark."

My body tensed.

"Get set."

I lifted my butt in the air and ignored how much it hurt my fingertips to hold my weight forward. I—would—not—fail.

"Go."

Though my intention had been to blaze down the track, leaving a fiery trail behind me, that idea quickly fizzled. Good God, when was the last time I'd actually run? I couldn't remember. A better tactic was to set a quick jog. Weird things happened as I made my way around the track. Over the years my body had morphed into something I didn't know. Areas of me jiggled that hadn't ever before. After the second bend in the track my muscles burned. Air fought its way into my lungs. The whole experience was pathetic.

With each step more of the bravado I'd felt at the starting line evaporated. I veered off the track and jogged toward the horse. The thing seemed taller. Not sure I'd make it over, I gave an extra bounce on the springboard. I realized my mistake too late. Pitching forward, I smashed into the horse. Luckily I gained enough height to roll over the top in a tangle of arms and legs. As I dropped onto the opposite side, my hand snagged under one of the handgrips.

"Sweet mother!" I stumbled to my feet, twisting my ankle, and yanked my hand free. A steady throb took root at the base of my palm. Rubbing the spot did nothing to physically soothe the injury, but it kept my cursing contained.

"You okay?" Nate walked toward me, but I stopped him.

"Fine." I limped toward the rope ladder. Pain continued to ripple through my wrist and ankle, but I tried my best to ignore it.

You can do this. You can do this.

Surprisingly, the ladder didn't pose much of a problem. My legs felt like they were on fire, taking a lot of my weight as I climbed, but at least I didn't flop around like a salmon in a net. With relative ease I scaled the web. The next phase was a different story.

Once at the top, I flailed for the wooden platform. Even by twisting my body, I just brushed the scaffolding with my fingertips. The only answer was to climb as high as possible and get above it. Medical bills started piling up in my mind. Broken wrist, sprained ankles, maybe even a broken back if I fell.

I glanced down. Nate stared at me, a hint of a smirk playing at his mouth. That was the motivation I needed.

I gripped the top rope and climbed until my feet were level with the plank. Extending my leg, I eased my left foot onto the ledge. From below I'm sure my position looked ridiculous, but at this point I didn't care. I'd finish this damn course or die trying. Okay, that was a little drastic, but the realization of how out of shape I was pissed me off. Just another thing that had fallen apart after Jeff's death.

Overhead, I grabbed the handle protruding from the scaffolding and pulled myself onto the ledge. The ground twenty feet below wavered, and I clung to the handle for dear life. I closed my eyes and waited for the world to stop spinning.

Note to self: Avoid heights if possible.

The ledge hadn't looked so narrow from below. Reluctantly I released my death grip and crouched. A belly crawl seemed like the best idea. Safe, low to the board, and less chance of falling. Inch by inch I made my way to the end of the ledge. The rope dangled in front and I latched onto it like a shark on a tuna. White knuckled, I stood.

Again, it had been my intention to ease onto the rope and lower myself to the trampoline. The second my full weight cleared the platform, my grip slipped. Fire race along the palms of my hands as I plummeted toward the trampoline. For somebody watching, I'm sure I looked like I knew what I was doing. My resonating scream however, quickly extinguished that notion.

My feet hit the knot at the end of the rope, cramming my knees into their sockets. Certain my hands were a bloody mess, I released my grip and dropped on all fours onto the trampoline. I bounced several times, biting my tongue. God, I hated this job. What was I thinking when I said I'd be a reaper?

After the momentum slowed, I struggled to my feet. Every part of my body hurt. If it hadn't been for Nate watching me, I would have lay there curled in a ball, whimpering. Testing my balance, I gave a couple of shallow bounces.

The smaller surface I was supposed to leap onto seemed a lot farther away than when we walked the course. Who designed this damn thing? Satan himself? I closed my eyes and took a deep breath. I was almost finished. I could do this. My lids slid open and my gaze focused on the projected landing spot.

With cat-eyed concentration, I bounced and launched. It felt like I lifted ten feet off the ground. The truth was probably more like I just cleared the trampoline. But I made it. Like a real gymnast, I stuck my landing.

Nate's brows lifted with surprise. *Suck it, reaper.*

Now pretty full of myself, I leapt off the trampoline, landing with a solid thud on the mat, and jogged to the balance beams. No problem. Hefting myself up, I skittered along the widest beam. I moved a little slower on the next one, but didn't fall. Though lower to the ground, the last and narrowest beam required my undivided attention and best balancing skills. My ankles shook from the effort it took to remain upright. What happened if I fell? God forbid I'd have to start again.

At the end of the beam I gave myself a mental high-five and jumped down. It would have been impressive if I'd sprinted the final lap of the track. Would have been, but I didn't. As a matter-of-fact, I'm not sure I could have called it a jog at all. My quick walk was interspersed with a few sluggish running steps, but then I'd have to slow again. My lungs burned and blood pounded in my head. Sweat poured off me as if I'd been doing an hour of heavy cardio. It was embarrassing and even more humiliating.

With the finish line a mere ten feet away, I found the

last of my energy and sprinted past Nate. I heard the click of his stopwatch.

"Not bad," he said.

I bent, bracing my hands on my knees and sucked in air. I'd never been super athletic, but I was wheezing like a two-pack-a-day chain smoker. "What's—" Cough. Pant. I could barely form words. "My time?"

"Seven minutes, ten seconds." Nate stopped in front of me. "You okay?"

I nodded, still unable to speak coherently. After another minute, I straightened. "Yeah, I'm great." Sweat dripped into my eyes and I wiped it away with the bottom of my sweatshirt. "So I passed?"

"Yep." He walked away. "The first round, anyway."

"What?" Surely I hadn't heard him correctly. I inhaled and blew out a long breath. "The first round?"

He stopped near a trunk and opened it. "That was just the first run. If you hadn't finished we wouldn't bother with the second heat."

The urge to wrap my fingers around his neck and squeeze intensified. I knew this testing wasn't his fault but he seemed to be enjoying it way too much. "But I already did it with over two minutes to spare."

Nate reached into the trunk and pulled out a bright orange, mesh jumpsuit. He gave it a couple of shakes, and then held it up for me to see.

"What the hell is that?"

"You'll wear this on your next run. It's meant to simulate transporting a soul." He indicated the sleeve for me to see. "There's Velcro at the cuffs and chest."

I stared at him, still not understanding. "How does Velcro simulate reaping?"

"Because…" Nate dropped the jumpsuit on the ground and dug in the trunk again. This time he extracted what looked like a life-sized pillow doll. "This will be attached to you."

If I understood him correctly he expected me to run the course I'd barely gotten through, with a gigantic pillow stuck to me. "That is the stupidest thing I've ever heard."

"Maybe, but it will give you a sense of what you'll be dealing with if you encounter a resistant spirit or difficult terrain."

Maybe I could get a job as a barista. I liked coffee and Danishes. What was a few scalding milk burns compared to this? Thinking about running the course again made my stomach lurch and my head pound harder. Doing it while lugging the pillow around made me want to cry defeat. Nate's expression made clear that's exactly what he expected. Though exhausted and slightly beaten down, I was not willing to except more humiliation. "Will I be timed again?"

The grin he'd barely concealed stretched across his mouth. "No. Take all the time you need."

What I needed was a long nap and a miracle. "I've got to pee."

He replied by pointing toward the locker room. Doing my best to stand tall and not limp, I brushed past him and headed across the gym. Pushing open the heavy locker room door hurt. Walking hurt. Thinking hurt. How I'd ever get through the course dragging a body pillow was beyond me.

I stopped at my locker and yanked it open. A full icy bottle of water sat in a puddle of condensation. Before taking a long drink, I rubbed the cool container against my forehead. The heartbeat pounding in my head eased a little but my lungs still burned. A piercing stitch set up residence in my right side. After opening the spout of my bottle, I squeezed the cold liquid into my mouth. What I wanted was to gulp down every drop but I knew I'd pay for it with a side-stitch once I started the course again.

After snapping the lid shut, I set the bottle on the top shelf and reached for the towel hanging on one of the hooks inside. A tiny jangle clanked at the bottom of the locker. My raven charm. I picked it up and held it in my palm. The metal warmed against my skin. After shoving it in my pocket the day the bird dropped it at my feet, I'd pretty much forgotten about it.

The edge of the tiny scythed glimmered blue. Maybe there was something to this bond I had with Fletcher. That's what I'd named him, getting tired of calling him the weirdo bird. At this point I could use all the help I could get, magical or otherwise. I unhooked my snowflake necklace and slid the raven charm onto the gold chain. It could have been my imagination but I swear tiny sparks flickered around the pendants when they touched. The metal was cool against my chest when I rehooked the chain and what felt like spider web threads of electricity rippled across my skin.

I rolled my shoulders and cocked my head side to side, suddenly feeling reenergized. If the charm did have magic, maybe it could give me an edge on the stupid obstacle course. Not taking any chances that Nate might call cheating if he saw the charm, I slipped it into the neck of my sweatshirt. Maybe there was hope yet. I slammed the locker closed, squared my shoulders, and strode back into the gym.

He glanced up from his cell phone, his eyes narrowing slightly. "You okay?"

"Great. Why?" Acting natural or the ability to lie weren't skills I'd been gifted with. Most of the time I over compensated. Usually my eyes were too round and innocent, or my voice raised an octave. "Don't I look okay?"

I'd totally set myself up for one of his insults, but it was a small sacrifice if he didn't figure out I wore the charm. For some reason Nate didn't take the bait. Instead he nodded. "You look good."

Maybe I was making an ego mountain out of a slip-of-the-tongue molehill, but I was fairly certain he'd just complimented me. Our gazes locked and a zing of sexual tension crackled between us. At least I think it was sexual tension. It had been a long time since I'd experienced it.

Even if he wasn't feeling the connection, it was nice to hear something flattering come out of his mouth for a change. And the little jitter that rocketed through me let me know I wasn't completely dead inside. Wow, I really needed to change the batteries in my vibrator if I was thinking about Nate in *that* way.

Dragging his gaze from me, he turned and busied himself with the jumpsuit. It suddenly felt very warm in the gym. The urge to fan myself was barely overridden by the intense desire to act as if his compliment hadn't stroked my comatose vanity.

"Put this on." He turned and shoved the jumpsuit at me. Guess cuddling was out.

My *I'm rockin' this reaper* bubble burst. I repressed a groan and lifted the orange abomination from his grasp. "I'm going to look like the Great Pumpkin in this."

He snorted. “Yeah.”

“You’re loving this.” I glared at him. “Aren’t you?”

“Oh yeah.” His head bobbed up and down. “But we’ve all had to wear it. So don’t think I’m torturing you needlessly.”

I harrumphed and sat on the gymnasium floor. Getting my tennis-shoed foot through the leg hole proved to be more difficult than the obstacle course. “What the heck.” The orange mesh caught on the treads of my shoe, not allowing me to shove my foot through or remove it. “I can’t…it’s wrapped around my toe.” I jammed my foot downward into the wall of mesh. That only succeeded in reinjuring my already sore ankle. After a few seconds, I gave a battle cry of fury and kicked my leg, trying to dislodge the jumpsuit. “Stupid firkin’ farkin’ piece of crap.”

Though the f-bomb rarely passed my lips, I’m not averse to connecting as many like-sounding F-words as I can when I get frustrated. Nate’s brows lifted as I continued muttering a string of F alternatives.

He let me struggled for another minute before he knelt and grabbed my foot, which I beat against the floor. “Stop.” He had my ankle in a vise grip, so I didn’t have any choice but to do as he said. “Next time take your shoe off first.”

“Next time?” I pointed and shook a finger at him.

"There's not going to be a next time."

"Then…" He tugged the jumpsuit from my foot. "I suggest you don't fail."

That was the best incentive he could have given me. No way did I want to endure another round of making a fool of myself—at least not here. My klutzy nature ensured I'd screw up at some point, but I wouldn't invite humiliation if I could help it. "Oh, I won't fail."

I yanked off my shoes and snatched the jumpsuit from Nate. Not only would I not fail, I'd kick this course's ass and call it girl names when I was finished. I stood and wiggled into the mesh. Though the jumpsuit was snug in places, it wasn't uncomfortable. Probably better tight than loose. That way I wouldn't get hung up anywhere. At least that was my hope.

After putting on my shoes, I stood. "Now what?"

Nate handed me the pillow person. It was heavier than I thought it would be, but nothing I couldn't carry.

"You must keep control of the soul at all times." He gripped my forearm and pointed to my wrist. "There's Velcro here." His fingers moved to press between my boobs. "And here."

A flurry of butterflies erupted in my stomach again, but he seemed oblivious to my reaction, or the fact that as co-workers he touched me inappropriately. I simply nodded, keeping my gaze pinned to his. "Gotcha."

When he lowered his hand, I cradled the pillow person, hugging it to me. Chest to chest, the Velcro connected. I let go and the pillow stuck. I did a few jumping jacks, but it didn't fall off. This would be easy. I didn't even have to hold onto it, leaving my hands free to climb and grip. A thought popped into my head. "Why the chest?"

"What do you mean?"

The rip of Velcro being peeled apart sounded as I pulled the pillow away from me. "I get sticking it to the wrists. It requires me to hold on, just like I did with Leroy Badder. But why at the chest?"

"If you embrace a soul and hold it against you, it will remain stuck. Like a heart-to-heart connection."

I scrunched my face, remembering how Leroy Badder's soul had cut though me like an icy blade, and I'd only touched him with my hands. "Ick."

"Not all souls are as nasty as Badder," Nate said, seeming to read my thoughts. "Most of your charges won't possess the dark aura or violent feel."

A shiver skittered up my spine. "Still." I shifted the pillow and connected it to the Velcro at my wrist. "I will never willingly do that."

He shrugged and checked his watch. "Your choice. We need to get started."

A sigh heaved from me and I murmured some incoherent objection that sounded a lot like Yosemite Sam.

I took my place at the yellow line on the track. To make sure I didn't drop the pillow during my run I gripped its mitten-shaped hand. And that was exactly the way I'd planned handling all my souls. The less contact the better.

"Whenever you're ready. Take all the time you need."

Since I wasn't being timed, I started out with a slow jog. This was going to be easy. Without the pressure of beating the clock I could finish this course in my own sweet time. As I rounded the first bend a loud scraping echoed through the gym. I glanced back up the track at Nate. He was moving what looked like a metal doorframe across the end of my lane, but I couldn't see exactly what it was. My good mood dipped. I knew simply running the course again would have been too easy.

I continued to watch him move from obstacle to obstacle. More scraping along the floor ricocheted around the gym as he pushed the springboard away from the pommel horse.

"Son-of-a…" I bit down the curse, realizing I'd have to climb over the apparatus instead of ungracefully springing over it.

At each obstacle he added a new hindrance. I

swallowed down my complaint and focused on the track ahead of me. Already I was out of breath and beginning to perspire. The pillow swished along the floor beside me. With each step it seemed to grow a little heavier. I really needed to dust off my treadmill and start working out.

My jog slowed and I stopped in front of the metal barricade. It was a turnstile on wheels, like something I'd see at airport security. Except this barrier was only about five feet high. The logical thing would be to connect the pillow to my chest, duck, and push past the metal bar, but I couldn't bring myself to do it. It was the principle of the matter. I understood the pillow was just a metaphorical soul, and wouldn't give me the sickening sensation Badder had—at least that's what I assumed. But I'd been naïve, taking Nate at his word. I thought I just had to run the course. Now here he was throwing up more obstacles. Any trust I'd had vanished, that included believing the pillow was just a pillow.

I eyed the barricade. Fine, I'd drag my burden through after me. Dipping my head, I walked forward and pushed against the bar blocking my way. At first it didn't give, so I leaned against it with all my weight. The bar rotated so fast I fell forward, but not before another bar snapped up and nailed me in the back. I gasped for air and stumbled. The pillow caught on the other side, nearly yanking my arm out of the socket.

"You and the soul must get through the turnstile."

"No shit, Sherlock," I mumbled under my breath. I tugged on the pillow, but one of the hands had lodged at the juncture of the rotating wheel. "Come on." I jerked on the material, but when ripping sounded, I froze. What would that mean if this were an actual soul? Would only part of the spirit get transported, leaving little bits of the soul stuck in different places like the subway or an electric can opener? "Shit."

I bent and peered into the cog of the turnstile. The fabric had hooked on a spring. I jiggled the bar, trying to maneuver it so I could slide the fabric free. Nothing budged. I poked my finger inside and pushed on the bar again. Pain shot through the tip of my finger. I gasped and yanked my hand free. A good size blood blister rose from the pad and instinctively shoved my finger into my mouth and sucked. I'm not sure why. It didn't ease the pain and actually caused the throbbing to intensify. I pulled my finger free and shook it wildly. Again, a stupid move, but I was pissed. I jerked the pillow as hard as I could.

More ripping, and the fabric sprang free—minus one thumb. "Sorry." I grimaced and poked the stuffing back into the hole where the thumb used to be. "Maybe you don't need fingers in Heaven."

I glanced up. Nate stared at me from across the gym but didn't say anything. I tucked the pillow under my arm and jogged toward the pommel horse. Half way across the floor, I stopped. "What the hell?"

"It's barbed wire." Nate walked toward me. "Get down and crawl through."

What was this, a war zone? "You're joking?"

"No. It's meant to simulate difficult terrain."

I propped one hand on my hip and let the other hang at my side, still gripping the pillow soul. "This is Alaska, not Afghanistan."

"You never know where you'll be assigned." He scribbled a quick note on the clipboard. "But we can stop and run the course again tomorrow if you want."

I straightened. "No way. I'm doing this now."

Despite my opinion about the ridiculously stupid course, I was big enough to admit that many times in my life I hadn't seen the big picture. And since I knew little to nothing about actual fieldwork as a reaper, I was willing to give Nate the benefit of the doubt.

Logic dictated I Velcro the pillow to my chest. Unfortunately my stubbornness usually kicked logic's ass when push came to shove. Hunkering down like I'd seen in war movies, I shimmied my body forward, dragging the pillow beside me.

The opening narrowed. What the heck? Did GRS have something against rubenesque women? Ropes of pointy wire crisscrossed above me, leaving only a few feet for me to maneuver. About a yard in the pillow snagged on a barb. Feeling the doll had given enough when it sacrificed its thumb, I wiggled backward and detached it. Again I moved forward and again it snagged. He cleared his throat with the kind of sound that covered a laugh. *Bastard.*

There was no way I was getting through this without shredding the pillow. Drastic measures were in order. Coming to the decision I'd rather suffer the sticky feel of a soul than Nate's condescending attitude, I shoved the pillow under me. The Velcro pads fused.

Though a little awkward, the pillow made moving a whole lot easier. Instead of shimmying, I was able to push my body forward, and slide along the polished floor. Even though the muscles in my arms quivered like a frightened Chihuahua, I felt pretty smug by the time I reached the end of the barbed wire enclosure.

I struggled to my feet, ungracefully clawed my way over the vault, and then shuffled to the wall of ropes. The doll bounced against me, its head bopping mine every time I took a step. I pushed it to the side but the pillow rebounded back and blocked my view. I grabbed the soft head and shoved it against my neck, clamping down with my chin.

That did the trick.

The rope wall spread out and up. My arm shook when I raised it to grasp the rope above my head. Stepping onto the lowest rung, I began my climb, making sure to keep all the weight on my legs. The trek was slow but I progressed nonetheless. Like I said, I would not fail. I sent up a silent "Thanks" when I reached the top. Nothing out of the norm had happened. Nobody dumped oil on me from above, or let loose a swarm of spider monkeys to attack me.

I turned my head to see where the ledge was located. The head of the pillow sprang free from my grip. "Crap." I stretched my neck, trying to contain it again, but couldn't reach. "Stupid—thing."

In such a precarious position I couldn't flatten myself against the wall to get ahold of the pillow's head. Each attempt caused my arms to shake. The possibility of tumbling to the ground became a very real threat.

Abandoning my efforts, I looked over my shoulder and extended my leg along the ledge. Nate hadn't climbed the rope ladder when sabotaging the course, so I hoped there were no hidden surprises for me on the narrow ledge. I shifted my weight and using the handle on the scaffolding again, eased onto the platform. Unlike the first run I couldn't hunker down. There was a big frickin' pillow in my way. But neither could I see around it. Again I crammed the stuffed head under my chin.

Inch by inch, I scooted along the wood, feeling my way with the toe of my shoe. Luckily there were no pitfalls. The rope hung in front of me, taunting me to grab it. Learning my lesson during my last run, I snaked it with my hand and wrapped the rope around my foot. I'd seen it done on TV, so I knew it had to work. Relief washed through me when I didn't zip to the bottom of the line.

Though awkward with the pillow attached to my chest. I slid down without injuring myself, and hopped onto the trampoline.

At this point the pillow became a growing hindrance. Sure it might break the fall if I missed the next trampoline, but it was tough keeping my balance. I yanked the pillow off my chest and attached it to my wrist again. Bounce-bounce, and I landed on the smaller trampoline.

The end was in sight. Only three balance beams and a trip around the track. I jumped down and mounted the first beam. The deep roar of a motor revved and suddenly a blast of air hit me from the right side, almost pushing me off. My body tilted to the left and my foot lifted.

"Ahhh!" I did one of those tottering *will she or won't she fall* stances. The wind cut off my breath.

Coherent words were impossible. The arm opposite my lifted foot shot out in an effort to not fall. It was only a about a yard drop, but to me it might as well have been a cliff. I hovered, my body splayed like a five-pointed star. The pillow lifted and I knew I was going over. Reaching deep, I dipped into the ninja skills lurking inside me, and lowered my foot to the balance beam. Thank God for ample hips. I shoved it into the wind, which brought me fully onto my narrow perch. Now balanced, I yanked the pillow to me and slammed it against my chest. Looking to my right I saw Nate standing next to a fan. The thing was ginormous. Why hadn't I noticed it before? Probably because I hadn't suspected treachery.

Refocusing on my course, I tucked the pillow head under my chin once again and scooted along the beam. At the end, I jumped down and mounted the next. The wind continued to batter me but I was too determined. At this point it could have been a fiery tornado and I wouldn't have fallen.

When I made it to the end of the last balance beam the wind stopped and the roar of the fan died. I didn't look at Nate. I was too close to conquering this *mutha* of an obstacle course. Jogging forward, I tensed, ready for anything he threw at me. But nothing happened. And when I crossed the finish line, Nate stood waiting with a genuine look of surprise, and might I say admiration on his face.

I stopped in front of him and dropped the pillow,

glaring at him. “Can’t handle being a reaper, eh? Well suck it, Cramer. Looks like you’ve got a new partner.”

With that I strode across the gym to the locker room. Yeah, there was a new angel of death in town.

CHAPTER ELEVEN

By six o'clock that night all my righteous indignation had evaporated into a mass of bruises, rope burns, and pulled muscles. A long, cylindrical black and blue patch stretched across my lower back where the turnstile had smacked me. And trying to remove my sports bra had turned into a painful wrestling match that left me lying on the bed, whimpering and defeated.

"Vella!" For once I was grateful for her casual attitude on dropping by at all hours of the day. "I need help." At that point I had no pride. All I wanted was a hot shower and if that meant exposing myself to my best friend, well, so be it. "Vella!"

The door to my bedroom sprung open. "What's wrong?"

I wiggled the arm I'd gotten free from the spandex torture. "Help."

"Oh my giddy aunt." She closed the door and walked

to the bed. "What happened?"

"I can't get out of my bra."

"I can see that. I mean where did you get all those bruises? You look worse than I did after the greased pig catching contest at the fair."

"I had to run the obstacle course today. Special stress on obstacle." I rolled to my back, one arm still pinned to the side of my head. "Everything hurts."

"Can you sit up?"

I rocked forward a couple of times, but the muscles in my stomach lit off a loud protest. "No."

"How about rolling to your side?"

"Noooo."

Vella propped a hand on her hip. "Can you lift both arms over your head?"

"Think of me as a vegetable. I am incapable of movement and thought at this point."

"All right." Vella held out her arms with her palms facing me. This meant she had an idea. Whether it would cause me excruciating pain was still to be seen. "I'm going to help you sit up. Then I'm going to work that sports contraption off you."

"K."

"I apologize right now if I happen to touch your boobs. Copping a feel is not my intention."

My boobs had seen a lot of action lately. Too bad none of it was of an amorous nature. "Noted."

After climbing onto the bed, she shoved her hands under my shoulders and hefted me into a sitting position. My groan morphed into a long moan. Each stomach muscle tightened and protested. Who knew I had so many muscles. From the pain radiating through me I swore I'd been born with twice the amount.

"I'm too young to be in this much agony." Another whimper squeezed from me. I'm not a very good patient. Kind of whiny.

"You need a long hot shower and an adult beverage to relax your muscles." Vella forced my arm down and through the chest band of the sports bra, popping me free from the spandex jail. With a quick swoosh, she yanked the garment off of me. Even my bra flab hurt. "Now lay back."

I tried to ease myself back but my quivering muscles were having none of it. I hit the bed like a falling boulder and bounced a few times. Vella climbed off the mattress and lifted my leg, extracting the running shoe. I lay there, bare breasted, unable to manage a modest arm across my chest.

"Lift your butt so I can get your pants off."

Right. Like that was going to happen. When I didn't move, she shook her head and yanked my yoga pants, dragging my undies with them. Okay, I wasn't hurting that much. I curled my fingers around their elastic waistband and held on. It had been a long time since anybody had seen me naked and if it was going to happen again, I didn't want it to be with my best friend.

A final tug and I was free from all my stretchy workout clothes. With great effort, I rolled to my side and pushed myself up. "You're a good friend."

"I know." Vella tossed the pile of clothes into my laundry basket, and then looked at me. She cocked her head. "For having three kids you've got some nice tits."

"As much as I appreciate the compliment, I don't want to talk about my boobs with you."

"I'm just saying, a lot of women don't keep their perk. You're lucky."

Ignoring her, I pointed to my open closet. "Robe, please."

She lifted my fluffy white robe from the hook and draped it over her arm. Then she held out her hands. "Up you go."

I locked fingers with her and allowed her to pull me to my feet. More pain radiated through me. What was the saying? The second day was always the worst. I couldn't imagine my body hurting more unless somebody set me on fire. "Thank you."

"Go take a hot shower and I'll fix something to eat."

She slid the wrap up my arms and settled it on my shoulders. "You should relax the rest of the night."

Pulling the lapel closed, I nodded. "Okay." I straightened and grimaced. "Thanks again for your help."

She waved me away. "Go."

I shuffled to the bathroom and locked myself inside. Turning the water on as hot as it would go, I dropped the robe and climbed in. Though I couldn't actually say the heat eased my pain, it certainly loosened some of the tightness.

My hand brushed the two pendants lying against my chest. I held them between my index finger and thumb, gently rubbing them. I wasn't convinced the raven charm had supernatural powers, but I was willing to invest a little effort to find out.

Forcing myself to relax, I concentrated on the charm and let the steaming water flow over me. After a few seconds the sensation of being stroked with feathers bushed across my skin. I continued to rub, enjoying the feel. The tension in my neck and shoulders eased. After another minute the sensation faded, taking with it, a little of my pain.

Jets of water pummeled my back. There was no doubt I still hurt, but not as much as before I'd entered the shower. Maybe there was more to the charm than I'd originally thought. Maybe there was still more to discover. I really hoped so since I didn't get everlasting beauty and strength when I became a reaper.

After twenty bliss-filled minutes the water turned cold. I shut off the shower, feeling a lot better. Another ten minutes found me in the kitchen, stomach growling, and throat parched.

Vella and Bronte were busy cutting up a variety of cheese, fruit, and vegetables, laying them on a platter.

"It looks like a snack-platter for dinner," I said. Truly, it was one of my favorite meals. Who didn't love hors d'oeuvres? It was like a party without all the work.

"Quick and easy," Vella said. She turned, holding the tray. My mouth watered. "I hope you don't mind me mixing up a little of my homemade salsa too."

"No, I love your salsa." My eyes cut to my daughter. "And you're helping?"

Bronte glanced up. "Yeah, I know you had a hard day."

Her smile was sweet and innocent, which put me instantly on alert. "That's so sweet of you to help." I shuffled to one of the chairs at the table and sat. "It really takes the pressure off knowing you're willing to pitch in." Bronte's smile tightened just a fraction. "And to do it out of the kindness of your heart, not expecting anything in return." My features slackened. "It really means a lot."

"Sure." The word rushed out, pitched a bit higher

than was natural. "We have to help out each other. Give and take."

"Exactly." I nodded, continuing to hold her gaze.

She blinked several times before looking back at the tray of cheese she was arranging. "But…"

Here it came. She wanted something. Rarely did Bronte do anything without a calculated reason. "But nothing," I said, cutting her off. "You're awesome. Best daughter ever."

"Yeah—yeah—that's true." She nodded. "I'm a pretty great daughter." Her head continued to bounce like a bobble-head doll. "Which is why you should let me go to Payton Alexander's Halloween party."

Okay, it wasn't as bad as I thought. "Who's Payton Alexander?"

Vella set a bottle of Corona in front of me. "Doesn't his daddy own the furniture store on C Street?"

"The guy who screams in his TV commercials?" I took a drink, stalling for time.

"Yeah, that's him, but Payton isn't creepy like that." Bronte placed several mouth-watering selections on a small plate and set it in front of me. A silent bribe to sway my vote. "Actually he's really shy."

"Cute?" Vella asked.

A flush crept across Bronte's cheeks, telling me

exactly what I needed to know. She shrugged. "Yeah, he's all right."

That meant gorgeous in Bronte lingo. "Huh." I took another drink, but didn't say anything.

"So, can I go?"

I stared at my daughter. "Who else will be there?"

"Fang and William."

Bronte's best friends. Fang was a cute little Chinese girl with a serious case of *the Goth*. Constantly dressed in black and skulls, she looked more like a reaper than I did. William was the nerd of nerds, but cute as all get out. I was fairly certain he had a crush on Bronte. Not that she noticed—or that she let on. "Is that all?"

"And Kelly Huff." Bronte continued to needlessly rearrange the bits of cheese on the tray. "She got her license and offered to drive us."

Red warning lights blared in my mind. "Kelly Huff? When did you guys become friends?" From what I knew of Kelly she was the most popular girl in tenth grade. Queen of the in-crowd. And a mean girl. She and Bronte butted heads a few times, so I didn't understand their new camaraderie. Then again, who really understood the mind of a teenage girl?

"We're not friends." Bronte plopped in the chair and bit into a cracker, chewed, and swallowed. "She likes

William."

"The Queen of Mean likes dear, sweet William?" Vella asked. "She'll eat him alive."

Bronte snorted. "Yeah, when I told him, he broke out in hives."

I traced the blue pattern ringing my plate. "I'm not sure I'm comfortable with you going to a party with a bunch of teenagers."

"Who else would I go with?" My daughter's head gave a little shake. The indignant kind that told me clearly I was an idiot. "I'm a teenager. My friends are teenagers."

The urge to tell her no pushed against my throat and it was difficult to repress. Trying to be reasonable, I bit back my retort. It wasn't that long ago I was in high school. The reason why everything seemed so important or monumental escaped me now, but I was trying to be understanding. "Will there be chaperones at the party? And by chaperones I don't mean older siblings. Parents, grandparents, a youth minster perhaps."

"I think his parents are going to be there or next door at another Halloween party." Bronte rested her arms on the tabled and leaned toward me. "Please? It's like, the first thing I've asked to go to since dad died."

Oh, she was good. Playing the dead dad card. Even though I couldn't argue the fact she'd basically been housebound for the past year, I still wasn't comfortable letting her go. "Let me think about it."

She groaned. "Come on, Mom."

"If you need an answer now, it'll be no." I leaned back in the chair and winced when the bruise on my back hit the wooden rungs. "But I promise I'll think about it."

She rolled her eyes and stood. "Fine." Turning, she skulked toward the door. "No matter what, I'm not trick or treating with Thing One and Thing Two this year."

"I didn't ask you to." My mom volunteered to take Bryce and Breck around her neighborhood. She was militant about checking Halloween candy for razor blades and straight pins. Plus, then I wouldn't have to shiver in the cold while my sons strategically hit every house within a five block radius. "Why don't you have your own party here?"

She stopped but didn't look at me. "What's the point? Everybody will be at Payton's party."

With that last jab of guilt, she left the kitchen. I sighed and took a long tug on my bottle. My daughter had never been into what was cool or following the popular crowd. It was one of the things I loved about her. From a very young age she'd marched to her own drum. It looked like those days were at an end.

Vella slid into Bronte's vacated chair. "You gonna let her go?"

"I don't know." I shook my head. "Teenagers, a party, and driving is never a good idea." Vella didn't have kids, but she had a ton of nieces and nephews. A few of them she'd practically raised. "Do you think I should?"

I expected some of her southern philosophy. Maybe something like, "You've got to let your kids kill their own rats." Instead she cocked her head and said, "Hell no."

"Why?"

"Besides the fact this Kelly Huff is obviously using Bronte to sink her claws into our sweet William, you've already lost your husband to a car accident. Do you really want to take a chance on your daughter's life? Especially with all the crazy people out on Halloween?"

Her words felt like a slap, but she'd voiced the exact concerns I'd been thinking. My memories of Jeff's accident were still so vivid they took my breath away. Imagining that with one of my children made me want to vomit. "No, I don't."

"She'll probably hate you for a while, but she'll get over it." Vella reached across the table and patted my hand. "The last thing you want is to reap your own child."

"Wow, you don't pull any punches." I gripped her hand and squeezed, letting her know I wasn't angry. "But you're right." I shook my head, searching for the right words. "I wouldn't come back from that."

Pulling her hand from mine, she sat back in the chair. "None of us would, Lisa."

Silence stretched between us. I popped another hunk of cheese in my mouth and chewed. Swallowing, I looked at her. "You're a good friend."

"I know." She lifted her bottle, drank, and then lowered it again. "You are too, despite this whole Angel of Death thing."

"Thanks—I think." Though the shower eased some of my aches, my body still throbbed. I sat forward and rolled my shoulders. "I'm not twenty anymore." I sighed. "What if I can't do this reaper job?"

"What's the worst that could happen?"

"Oh, I don't know. I could be killed or maimed." I hesitated. "Or humiliated." I rubbed my hands over my face. "God knows I've already done that enough."

"Listen." Vella tapped her bright pink nail on the table. "This might not be the best situation or your dream job, but it's going to put food on the table. Hell, I'd let you come work for me, but business has been slow."

Though Vella was my best friend, the thought of working at her hair salon, listening to Jonathan gossip all day made the hair on my neck prickle. At times I wasn't sure how Vella and I became such good friends. I didn't care about celebrity gossip, make up, or name brands. Because of her husband's high position at the oil company, she was involved in a lot of charities and social events. Whereas, I attended hockey games and constructed paper-mache turkey heads for school plays. We were the epitome of opposites attracting. I think that's why we worked.

"Thanks." I propped my elbows on the table, not wanting to put pressure on my back. "You're right. At this point I need to tough it out." I attempted a cheery smile. "Who knows, maybe I'll be the best reaper this side of the Arctic…once I stop hurting."

"Have another beer. It will help cure what ails you."

"I doubt it. Besides, I need a good night sleep tonight." My cheery smile tightened into a humorless grin. "God only knows what's in store for me tomorrow."

"Did Nate give you any clue?"

"Only that we *hit the seventh*. I hope that's not some metaphorical term for one of the circles of Hell."

"Well if it is, give my Uncle Donny Jo a message from me. Tell him I did not end up pregnant by Al Ambler. Nor did I have to resort to mud wrestling or lap dances to get through college." She took a swig of beer and then set it on the table with more force than necessary. "Oh!" She jabbed a finger at me. "And tell him Aunt Edith knew all along he was cheating on her with Alvaretta Hunt—though that's not what we called the woman."

"Yeah, I got it." A shiver skidded up my spine. "Hopefully, I won't meet Uncle Donny Jo or any other of your relatives tomorrow. Or ever."

"Well, if you do, don't turn your back on them." She pinned me with a gaze and nodded her head. "I'm just sayin'."

Hell just got a whole lot scarier.

CHAPTER TWELVE

At exactly ten the next morning I pushed through the front door of GRS. Nate leaned next to the elevator, thumbing through the Anchorage Newspaper. I straightened, trying to hide any indication that yesterday's training torture left me nearly incapacitated.

"What are you doing down here?" I stopped at the elevator and punched the button. "Afraid I wouldn't show up this morning?"

"The thought had crossed my mind." He smiled and folded the newspaper, tossing it into the recycle bin. "But—" He patted me on the back. Pain shot from my shoulder and down my back, nearly forcing a groan from me. I ground my teeth together to prevent a whimper from escaping. "I knew you were made of stronger stuff."

"Yep." I stepped away from him. "That's me. Tough as nails."

The elevator doors slid open and he held up his hand.

"After you—partner."

Was that sarcasm? It was difficult to tell with him sometimes, so I just assumed it was. "What fun things do we have planned for today?" I leaned against the back wall of the elevator. "Torture with hot pokers. Shoving toothpicks under my fingers. Five hours of being licked by cats while strapped to a chair?"

"What's the matter?" He slid his key card along the slot and pressed the number seven-button. "Yesterday too much for you?"

"No." Pasting on a sweet smile, I crossed my arms, ignoring that ache that emitted around the area of my bra flab. Until last night I hadn't realized I had muscles there. "But since I passed, and I'm here today, I thought you might have some new challenges for me."

The doors squeezed shut and he turned to face me. "Tests are over. Today you see Command Central and meet some of the higher ranking members of GRS."

"Sounds fun." At least the idea of a tour did. I wasn't sure what I would have done if he told me I had to lift or climb something. My stomach did a little flip when the elevator began to climb. "By higher ranking, do you mean reapers?"

"Reapers, command personnel—and others."

And others sounded ominous but I didn't question

him further. Once we reached the seventh floor, I'd find out what *others* were. No sense in stirring up my suspicious nature more than it already was. "Cool."

We rode the rest of the way in silence. I tried to appear unfazed by what waited for me on the seventh floor, and Nate seemed determined to break my calm façade by burning a hole in the side of my head with his stare. I ignored him. After another few seconds the elevator lurched and the doors opened.

It took all my will not to gawk at the sight. One large room spread out in front of me. Smoky colored floor-to-ceiling windows soared up the front wall, letting in the bright October sun. Raised voices, printers churning out copies, and the frantic tapping of keyboards whizzed around us.

"Ladies first." Nate indicated I should lead.

I stepped onto the blue carpet but didn't advance. The room reminded me of the bridge on a space ship. Computers lined one of the walls and in the center of the room was a circular elevated platform. What looked like radars pinged, registering tiny green blips on the screens. But it was the man standing in the center who drew my attention.

Yowza! I didn't think men like him existed in real life. The dark gray t-shirt he wore stretched across his broad back, and his biceps rolled from under the tight armholes. The fabric clung to his body and dipped into a pair of gray camouflage pants that hugged a rear end that made my fingers itch to touch it. I blew out a long, silent breath but didn't fan myself. I did have some control.

"This is Command Central. It's the heart of GRS," Nate said.

Not pulling my gaze from the mouth-watering Adonis, I pointed. "Who's that?" Nate snorted and with great difficulty, I looked at him. "What?"

"That's Constantine." A smirk turned up the corner of his lip. "He always gets that reaction."

"What reaction." I tried to play innocent but knew I was busted.

"The slack jaw, hypnotic gaze, and the fact that even though you're standing in the command center of GRS, all you can focus on is him."

"I am not…slack jawed." The rest of it? Guilty. "But seriously, you should have his picture on the recruiting pamphlet. I wouldn't have hesitated signing up."

At that moment Constantine turned. "Nate." He hopped off the platform. "And Lisa Carron, our newest recruit." He held out his hand. "I'm sorry for the circumstances of you being here, but I'm glad to have you."

"And I'm glad to be had—here, I mean."

Forget his silver gray eyes that seemed to glow, his silky voice, or the thick black hair that begged my fingers to run through it, my knees nearly buckled when I grasped his hand. A jolt of electricity shot through my body, warming me from my toes to the tips of my ears. Maybe it was a reaper thing, a way to acknowledge each other without acknowledging each other. Whatever it was, I'd be shaking his hand whenever possible.

He released me and hooked his thumbs on his front pockets. "Nate said you breezed through the obstacle course yesterday."

I highly doubted those were the words Nate used. "Breezed, stumbled, the main thing is I made it."

"Exactly. Come on, I'll show you around."

Oh happy day. Constantine walked to the center of the room, giving me another glimpse of his rear end. I followed in his wake. Damn he smelled good. If Heaven had a scent it would smell like this guy. My heart skipped a beat and I silently sighed. It was one of those *he's so dreamy* sighs, usually saved for teen heartthrobs.

"This is our tracking station." He pointed to the blipping radars. "It's where we monitor impending deaths."

Several green dots blinked on the screen, drawing my attention away from my incredibly hot superior. Some of the blips were bigger than the others. My stomach clenched at the idea those were people, going about their daily lives, unaware their time on Earth was counting down.

"Tempting, isn't it?" Constantine asked.

I glanced at him. "What is?"

"Wanting to rush out." His gaze held mine. The man must have read minds. "Warn them."

"Yeah, it is." No point in lying. "Does anybody ever do that?"

"It's happened, but it doesn't help."

The need to know battled with my knowledge that ignorance was bliss, and won. "Why not?"

"Only guardian angels can interfere. If a reaper tries to prevent the death it will still happen. Maybe not in the way planned, but it will still happen."

"That's depressing." I admit I had toyed with the idea of preventing some of the deaths I would encounter. But what was the point if the person ended dying anyway—maybe horrifically?

"Depends on how you look at death, I guess." Constantine stepped around me. "No doubt your opinion of it will change in time."

My eyes cut to Nate. "Did your opinion change?"

He nodded. "Oh yeah."

Before I had time to ask him how, Constantine pointed to a large, digital board hanging on the wall. Names were lit in green, and a series of yellow boxes glowed behind them. "These are the reapers stationed here in Alaska."

I noticed my name at the bottom of the list. Only one box was lit. "There's a lot more than I thought." Nate was in the number one spot with a string of yellow lights behind his name. "What do those mean?"

"Each light represents a reaped soul. Everybody has a quota for the year."

"Why do I have a box?" I hadn't reaped yet and figured it was some kind of confidence building tactic.

"Roy Badder," Nate said behind me.

"I didn't reap him." Sure, I'd touched him, but Nate did all the heavy lifting. Plus it was an accident. So I didn't feel I deserved the credit. "I just held onto him."

"Same thing," Constantine echoed what Nate had said in the Holiday bathroom.

"So, it's like a scoreboard?"

"Exactly. Soon you'll be up there with Nate."

My gaze skated up the list of reapers. God, I hoped not. Trying to infuse my voice with awe, I widened my eyes. "Impressive."

Nate grunted. "Right."

Okay, so maybe sincerity wasn't my best attribute when it came to him.

"Anyway," Constantine continued, "see the blinking square at the end of Edgar Cramdon's quota?" I nodded. "That means his client is dead but hasn't been reaped yet."

I shifted my weight to my other foot and crossed my arms over my chest. "Dead? For how long?"

"Not sure." Constantine took out his phone and scrolled through several screens. "Eighteen hours."

"Aren't we supposed to reap right away?" I couldn't imagine some poor soul being stuck while their body assumed room temperature. "I mean—it seems the considerate thing to do."

"Normally, yes." He shoved his phone back in his pocket. "But it was a suicide."

"What difference does that make?"

"It's not policy, so don't quote me on it, but we let suicides cool their heels before letting them cross over. Then maybe they'll think twice about taking their life the next time around."

There was a whole lot of information coming at me. Not *here's the break room and the pudding in the fridge belongs to Lois* information. This was secret of the universe stuff. "What do you mean—next time?

"Reincarnation," Constantine said as if he'd just said something as generic as muffin or socks.

"So…we come back?" Duh, he'd just said that, but it was the most intelligent thing I could manage while my brain drank the information. "By choice?"

"Of course. How else would you learn lessons?" He

smirked, revealing a dimple I hadn't noticed. "Walk in another man's shoes, so to speak."

"So I've reincarnated before?" Of course my imagination instantly shot to a princess or Gandhi.

"Absolutely." He walked to the closest computer terminal and typed in some information. "Let's see when and who you were."

"Get out of here." All of my inhibitions evaporated. I joined him, leaning close to him in an effort to see the monitor. "Are you googling this?"

"More like ethereal Googling. This computer connects directly to the Akashic Records."

"I've heard of those. They contain everything that's happened in history, right?"

He turned his head and smiled at me. "Very good."

I smiled back, which was a better option than acting on my impulse to run my tongue along his lips.

"In a nutshell, the Akashic Records chronicle every second of every hour in history since time began."

"Every second?"

His eyebrows lifted and he nodded.

"So drunk dialing my college ex incident?"

"Recorded. Sorry."

"Crap." I turned my attention to the computer monitor. "So who was I?"

"Let's see, a Mesopotamian priestess."

"Really? I hadn't expected something so glamorous."

He grimaced. "But you were sacrificed on the altar."

"I wasn't a virgin, was I?"

"Yeah." His gaze cut to me again. "Sorry."

"Figures. What else?" Surely not all my lives had ended so…unsatisfactorily.

"A Hebrew slave in Egypt. You were crushed by one of the pyramid blocks. A goat herder in Persia. Starvation."

"Starvation?" I wasn't sure how the whole reincarnation thing worked but I couldn't imagine not having had the same driving need to eat as I did today. "Why didn't I just eat my goats?"

Constantine gave a nonchalant shrug. "Don't know. Details are sketchy." He refocused on my life data. "You were also a Civil War soldier, a rice farmer in Asia, a milk maiden in eighteenth century Europe, and…oh." He pointed to the screen. "A prince to England's monarchy."

"Now that's what I'm talking about. Which prince was I?"

"Uh." His brow furrowed. "Henry the Eighth's son."

My excitement plummeted. "Wait, he didn't have any sons that lived, right?"

"Yeah, you died at birth."

"Figures." I straightened. "Okay, as fascinating as

this is, perhaps too much information isn't a good thing." I'm sure there were deep spiritual reasons why most of my past lives ended tragically, or seemed completely mundane. Maybe that was the equivalent of building character. "Now I understand why we don't remember our past lives. Actually I'm grateful. So depressing."

"Not everybody can be Cleopatra," Nate said. "The world needs goat herders too."

"Comforting." Anxious to move on, I clapped my hands together and rubbed. "What's next?"

"The rules." Nate picked up a thick book off the counter. At first I thought it was a phonebook. He shoved it at me. "Read it. Learn them."

"All of it?" I took the regulations from him. "Will there be a test?"

"Yeah, every time you reap a soul. That's your test," Nate said.

"I can't take this home. Somebody might see it." I looked at Constantine. "Aren't I supposed to keep my reaperhood a secret?"

"Yes." Constantine took the book and handed me a phone. "That's why we use this instead." A short huff of laughter escaped him and he shook his head. "Nate prefers an old school approach when it comes to training."

"Is this mine?" A shot of excitement raced through

me. The phone I held was several versions newer than the dinosaur I'd been using the last four years.

"All yours," Constantine said. "It's important that we're able to reach you when needed." He stood behind me and reached around my arm. His biceps rubbed against my upper arm. "This is the GRS app." He tapped on the tiny skull icon. "All the information you need is in here."

I nodded, but was having a hard time concentrating. "Where are the regulations?"

He tapped the documents tab, and then *Regulations and Procedures.* "Most of the stuff is common sense. Don't tell you friends about GRS. You've got to reap the soul you're assigned to. No afterlife messages to loved ones."

I craned my neck and looked at him. "Really? Why not."

"The chance of exposure are too great. People start asking questions. Pretty soon the grieving wife is on your doorstep, begging you to find out where the life insurance policy is."

"Oh." I looked back at the phone. "It just seems like a nice courtesy we could provide."

Having some afterlife message from Jeff would have definitely helped with the grieving process. Something along the lines of, "Thanks for being such a great wife. Tell the kids I love them." Or maybe, "By the way, you're next in line to be a grim reaper, so maybe stay out of the Holiday gas station if you don't want to pursue that line of work." What I got was radio silence.

"It's not," Nate said. "So get the idea out of your head."

"I didn't say I was going to do it," I argued, pretending that I hadn't just been thinking of ways around this rule.

"You didn't have to. I'm beginning to read your body language and you were definitely thinking about it."

I ignored him. Nate didn't know me, and he wasn't the boss of me. "Moving on," I said, dropping the phone into my pocket.

"Moving on," Constantine echoed. "Let's have a look at Purgatory."

"Purgatory?" I followed him, skipping a few steps to catch up. "You mean *the* Purgatory?"

"Yes and no." He pressed a button on the wall and two doors slid open. "They're containment cells used until the soul can be delivered. So, in a way it's Purgatory. Every command center has one."

We stepped into the room. A low hum buzzed across my skin. "What is that?" A shiver raced through me. "It's making the hair on my neck stand on end."

"That's from the ectoplasmic barriers."

"Pretend English isn't my first language."

He looked at me. "It's magic."

"See, that I understand," I said, walking forward. "But I thought we gave spirits to our porters."

"Most are, but in some cases their fate is undecided, so they have to hang out here a while." Constantine stopped beside me. "You shouldn't have this problem though. All your reaps will go through your porter."

"Speaking of which." I crossed my arms. The action was done more out of dread than confidence. I wasn't sure I was ready for a one-on-one with my porter. Pick had been uber creepy, and knowing me I'd get someone even freakier. "When do I meet mine?"

"No time like the present," Nate said from behind me.

He sounded a little too gleeful. I was instantly suspicious. "Will I have the same porter as Jeff?"

"That's doubtful." Constantine pressed the button and closed us inside Purgatory. "He's probably been reassigned since there was a year between Jeff and you."

With a deep breath, I faced him and circled my shoulders, as if preparing to spar. I circled my head and leveled my gaze in front of me. "Let's do this."

"For the initial meeting all you need to do is call for your porter," Nate said.

"Like when you called for Pick?"

"Exactly." He pulled out his phone and pointed it at me.

"What are you doing?" I asked.

A wicked grin split his face. "I want to capture your expression when you see your porter for the first time."

Jackass.

I jabbed an accusing finger at him. "What about the no tell rule? You can't show the picture to anybody."

"I can't show non-GRS employees. However, I can post it on our inter-office web page."

I looked at Constantine, my finger remaining aimed at Nate. "Can he do that?"

"Yeah, sorry, it boosts employee morale." He patted me on the shoulder and another zing of electricity shot through me. I flinched and scowled. "And I'm sure this won't be the last time he captures *the moment.* Nate loves this shit."

I lowered my arm but continued to glare at my partner. "Okay, but remember, two can play that game."

"Bring it on." His gaze captured mine. Clearly he didn't think I had revenge in me. Ha, the joke was on him. I had kids. Conniving was my middle name. "Are you going to call or should we go home for the day?" he continued.

"I kind of like the idea of calling it a day."

"Not an option," Constantine said, putting an end to our bickering. "Now, if you'd be so kind."

Determined to show Nate I was made of stronger stuff than he believed me to be, I took a big breath and called, "Porter."

Nothing happened.

Constantine shifted, crossing his arms. "Try again."

Even his simple request sounded like a command. Again, a tiny niggle of doubt that he was just a reaper ghosted through me. I cleared my throat. "Porter."

My heartbeat sped up when a thin pink line of light appeared at the end of the room. Instantly, I cued in on the pink and a tiny wave of relief washed through me. I hadn't considered I might get a female porter. The tension eased from my posture.

Just like at the Holiday station, the light widened and spread, forming a door. I glanced at Nate, but the jackass still had his phone pointed at me. I ignored him and turned back to the dimming light. Seconds ticked by as the scene solidified. For some reason I couldn't blink or look away. It was like opening a secret Santa gift at an office party. Would it be something good or a gag gift? After what seemed like forever, the door slid open.

Nate's camera clicked to my right a few times, but I was unable to look away from what I could only describe as the biggest gag gift ever. I pointed. “What—the hell—is—that?”

CHAPTER THIRTEEN

Well, it certainly wasn't a woman, but I wasn't sure it was a man either. *Creepy transvestite circus master* came to mind. Its yellow eyes peered at me over the top of small round sunglasses. Tall and thin, its stance was almost feminine. A shiny gold blouse draped its torso and bright purple leopard leggings hugged long, slender legs. The only masculine thing about the porter was the heavy heeled black boots. Spikes jutted from the sides and chains circled the ankles. Definitely a deterrent for getting too close—like I needed another reason not to get near this…porter.

"Oh crap," Constantine said.

I whipped around to face him. "Crap what? Why crap?"

"You've got to be kidding me," Nate added. I spun to him. He lowered his phone-camera. "This can't be right."

"Oh my God, would somebody tell me what's going on!"

"That's—"

"Hal Lee Lewya," the porter cut in with a deep purr. Okay, I went with male. He gave a low bow. "At your service, pretty lady." Hal straightened and smiled. A single gold canine winked at me, making him look like a 1980's music video star. "And you must be my new reaper." He tipped a tiny purple top hat in my direction. "A pleasure to finally be reassigned."

"More like a surprise you've been reassigned," Nate said.

"Why?" My gaze bounced between Constantine and Nate. "Why a surprise?"

"Hal had a little trouble with his last reaper." Constantine took a step forward, partially blocking my view. "Decided to take him on a little trip to Hell."

"What do you mean?" I remembered Nate telling me not to touch Pick. The reason was sinking in. "Like *Black Friday at Target* trip to Hell or literally a trip to *Hell*?"

"Literally—" Constantine let the rest of his statement hang, unspoken.

Hal waved a bejeweled hand in the air. "You got him back. I don't know what the big fuss was."

The floor shifted almost imperceptibly under my feet. My heart jumped to my throat. Earthquakes in Alaska are common, but I still hated them. I glanced at Nate. With a flick of his hand he motioned me closer. Seemed like a good idea for protection's sake. Obviously there was a lot going on I didn't understand.

"The big fuss is that," Constantine said, "he's spent the last nine years in a mental institution because of what he saw. And this isn't the first time you've pull a stunt like this, or do you need reminding?"

When Constantine spoke his voice was set low. Power rolled off him, as if emitting an invisible electrical charge. The light on the wall flickered. I took another step toward Nate. For the first time, I really looked at Constantine. Not just his chiseled body and stunning face, but all of him. I assumed he was nothing more than a GRS bigwig. Now I wasn't sure he was even human. The way Hal Lee Lewya cast his gaze toward the floor told me I was probably right.

"No, you don't need to rehash my sins. I assure you, Constantine, I have learned my lesson and have been thoroughly punished." Hal lifted his stare. "Enough to satisfy even you."

"I doubt that."

Silence blanketed the room. Unsure what I should do, I cleared my throat. That drew everybody's attention. "Soooo, is Hal my porter,"—which I seriously hoped he wasn't—"or am I to be assigned somebody new."

“No.” Constantine looked at me. “He’s yours.” He paused. “Sorry.”

Oh goodie.

I was learning that things at GRS were what they were, and there wasn’t a lot I could do about it. “Well then…” I turned to Hal. “My name is Lisa Carron.”

Hal’s yellow eyes drifted slowly down my body and back up to rest on my face. Okay, I needed a shower after that little perusal, but I ignored his rudeness. Or maybe he wasn’t being rude. Maybe a thorough body scan was considered proper behavior for one of the Netherworld’s minions. At that point I didn’t care. I just wanted him gone.

His long slim fingers toyed with a wide metal cuff at his wrist. “Lisa.”

The velvety purr of his voice wrapped around me and tugged me forward. I stepped toward him, but Nate grabbed my arm. My gaze tracked from his hand to face.

“Going somewhere?” he asked.

“What?” It took a couple of seconds for the situation to register. “I mean...” I glared at Hal. “That wasn’t very nice.”

He shrugged. “A little porter humor.”

“What, luring me in so you can drag me to Hell too?”

“You hurt me.” He pressed a delicate hand to his gold shirt. “I told you I’d learned my lesson.”

“No,” I pulled my arm out of Nate’s grasp, “you said you’ve been punished. It’s not the same thing.”

He tilted up his chin and laughed. “You’re clever, Lisa Carron.” Slowly his laughter died. “I will remember that.”

Unsure what he meant, I looked at Constantine. “Are we done here?”

“Yes, I think that’s quite enough for today.”

I looked at Hal again and mimicked Nate’s dismissal of Pick. “Our transaction is complete.”

With that, Hal bowed and stepped backward into the elevator. “Until next time, Lisa Carron.”

Again the urge to move forward gripped me but this time I was ready. It took all my will, but I remained rooted to my spot. The doors closed, swallowing Hal and releasing me from his compulsion. I slowly turned to face the boys. “Okay, would somebody please tell me why I’ve got a psychopath for a porter?”

“I wish I could, Lisa.” Constantine ran his fingers through his thick hair, worry etching his face. The locks fell back into place, but I didn’t find them so alluring this time. “I’ll check into it and let you know.”

“He’s dangerous,” Nate said. My gaze cut to him. “I know I give you a hard time, Carron, but I’m serious when I say you can’t handle him.”

Normally I would have bristled at the insult, but not this time. “No argument here.” I rubbed my arms, trying to chase away the lingering effects of Hal’s creepy impulse touch. “Don’t reapers have some kind of talisman against their porters? Maybe a magic potion I can drink every day?”

“There are a few things but they’re rare,” Constantine said.

“Like what? I’m willing to try anything.” Whatever I had to do to keep out of Hal’s reach, I’d do. “Eat eye of newt. Circle a grave three times at midnight on All Hallow’s Eve. Paint myself green and hop around in the front yard, naked. No matter what it is, I’m all in.”

“It’s not a matter of doing something as it is having something done to you.”

The thought of Constantine doing something *to* me sent a thrill, and a little apprehension, racing along. Until I’d seen, or more like, felt his power, I would have been all over him like a cheap suit. A little of my bravado fled. “It doesn’t hurt, does it?”

“Not usually.” Constantine gripped the back of his neck and rubbed. “On rare occasions a reaper will acquire an ally.”

I shook my head, not understanding.

“Someone or something adopts them, helps out in little ways. Maybe guides them.”

"You mean like a sidekick?"

"More like a familiar," Nate said. "You don't happen to have one of those…do you?"

Automatically my hand went to my neck, searching for the raven charm. I mentally cursed myself for having forgotten my necklace on the bathroom counter this morning. "Maybe."

Constantine stopped massaging his neck. "You do?"

"I don't know. There's this raven named Fletcher. Well, that's what I named him. Anyway, he's been following me around, sitting in the trees outside my house." I shrugged. "And maybe he gave me a raven charm."

"I take it you didn't bring the charm with you today?" Constantine asked.

"Yeah, how'd you know?"

"It's an amulet that will protect you. If you had it on, Hal's compulsion wouldn't have worked on you."

"Well, luckily Fletcher adopted me, otherwise…" The idea of being at Hal Lee Lewya's mercy sent a ripple of dread that wrapped around my bones and squeezed. I swallowed hard.

"Luck has very little to do with this." Constantine pressed the button on the wall and the doors to Command Central slid open. Before leaving Purgatory he looked at me. "It seems somebody is looking out for you, Lisa."

I blew out a long breath. “It’s about time,” I mumbled.

Nate moved up behind me. “Why don’t you go home and get that raven charm?” He stepped past me. “Put it on and don’t take it off—for anything.” I nodded. “Take the rest of the day off and rest up.”

“I’m fine. I don’t need to rest up.” The excitement of Hal Lee Lewya’s arrival had anesthetized yesterday’s soreness. At his words, all my aches returned. “I can get my charm tonight.”

“Better to go home and take it easy.” After stepping through the door Nate turned to me. “Tomorrow is Halloween. It will be one of your busiest nights of the year.”

“My busiest night?” I followed him across Command Central. “Why?”

“Halloween and idiotic stunts go hand in hand. Someone is bound to die.” He flicked his head toward the platform. “Have a look.”

A plump woman dressed in a violet pantsuit sat at one of the radars. We approached and I could see a dozen dots jumping around the screen. “Those aren’t all mine, are they?”

The woman turned and smiled up at me. “No honey, just this one, this one, and…” She pointed a purple painted nail at a large green blip. “This one.”

"Three?" I said.

"So far." She laughed. "But the day is still young."

She seemed to really love her job. "Do we know who they are?"

"I do." She turned back to the radar. "But you won't find out until the information is sent to your phone tomorrow afternoon. No sense flaunting temptation in your face."

"Oh, yeah." Despite already knowing this, I felt like a chastised child. "Of course."

"So go home and I'll see you tomorrow." Nate wrapped his fingers around my arm and guided me toward the door.

"But—" I wasn't sure why I was protesting. Probably because it felt like I was being shuffled out the door, and everybody seemed to have another agenda but me. "There must be something I can do around here."

"Nope." He gave me a little push into the elevator. "Not a thing." Reaching inside the elevator, he pushed the ground floor button. As the doors closed, he smiled and gave a little wave. "Have fun."

I returned a tight smile, but went willingly. Far be it from me to stay where I wasn't wanted, or to refuse time off. More than likely Hal Lee Lewya was the cause of being herded out of GRS, and truth be told, I'd rather have them taking care of that issue without my help. Nothing I could really do about it anyway. I didn't have pull or a clue as to what was going on most of the time.

On the way home, I realized I didn't have one errand to run or any pressing tasks that needed to be completed. Even the house clean and the laundry was done. So, I took an afternoon nap. Twenty minutes had been my goal, but two hours later I woke to the sound of my sons' pounding footsteps.

"Mom," Bryce bellowed, "we're home!"

No kidding. "I'm in here." I swept the blankets aside and swung my legs over the side of the side. The boys bound down the hall and launched themselves onto the bed. I bounced several times, laughing. "Have a good day?"

"Tomorrow's Halloween." Breck stood and gave two powerful jumps. "Candy."

"I can't wait," Bryce said, throwing his arms around my neck. After that declaration he jumped to the next subject. "What's for dinner?"

I broke his hold and stood. Cooking was the last thing I felt like doing. Actually, reaping was, but cooking came in a strong second. "How does fast food sound?"

A unanimous "Yay," erupted from both.

"Is your sister home?"

"Yeah, she's watching TV downstairs," Bryce said, taking a flying leap off the bed.

"Get ready. We leave in five," I called to his departing back.

Breck followed his brother, performing the same launch and run sequence. I stopped in the bathroom, fluffed a bit, and went to find Bronte. Like Bryce had said, I found her downstairs, snuggled into our big, red beanbag chair. Though she'd taken off her coat, she still wore her favorite black knit hat that had cat ears and a skull and crossbones on the front. She didn't look up when I entered.

"Hungry?"

She answered with a noncommittal grunt and a shoulder shrug.

"Fast food. Grease and sugar," I said, trying to coax a reaction from her. Her gaze never wavered from the television. Usually I'd get a cursory glance, but not even a blink in my direction. "What's wrong?"

"Can I go to Payton's Halloween party?" she asked, still not looking at me.

The party had completely slipped my mind. Ever since Jeff died, saying no had become difficult. I didn't like to deny the kids something fun, but I the thought of her going to the party gave me a bad feeling. First off, I didn't like Kelly Huff. Girls like her bullied or fluttered their eyelashes to get their way. In school I'd gotten the bullying end of the deal. Though I wanted Bronte to make her own mistakes, this one could get her hurt or worse. I didn't beat around the bush or try to cushion the letdown. "No. I don't trust Kelly to be a responsible driver."

She rolled her eyes and crossed her arms. "I knew you wouldn't let me."

"Then you shouldn't be disappointed." When she didn't reply, I tried another tactic. "Why don't you and Fang have a sleepover? It'll be fun. Invite a couple of girls. I'll be going out for a while so you'll have the house to yourself. Watch a scary movie and eat junk food."

She looked at me. "Where are you going?"

To reap at least three souls. I went with my standard answer. "Vella's." She grunted again and I took it to mean my night would be lame. Better her think that than know the truth. "Come on." I held out my hands. "Let's eat, then we can discuss your plans for tomorrow night."

She stared at my hands for a few seconds and finally sighed. Grasping her fingers, I pulled her to a stand and into my arms, wrapping her in a tight mom hug. Even though she stood there, arms limp at her side, she turned her head and laid her cheek against my shoulder. Obviously she wasn't that mad.

***

McDonald's was packed. Obviously a lot of other parents hadn't felt like cooking either. The boys made a beeline for the play area, while Bronte and I ordered. After our food arrived, we carried it into the kid zone. Instantly, I was struck by the smell of the cleaning fluid they used. A little Pilipino woman wove her way through the patrons, wiping a table here, sweeping up spilled fries there, and keeping the place clean as clean as possible with so many kids around.

The noise level was ten times that of the adult section beyond the glass. I envied the childless people. Sitting and eating without screams of small children piercing their skulls. We commandeered the corner table, and after brushing sprinkles of lettuce off the bench, slid onto the bright red laminate seats.

I doled out the food, prepping the boys' kid's meals for their dine-and-dash dinner habits. Bronte was plugged into electronic life support, completely ignoring me, so I pulled out my new phone and thumbed through the screens. Several icons for GRS scrolled by. I tapped on the skull and went to Rules and Regulations. Man, there were a lot of them. How was a person supposed to learn all these?

It is prohibited to purposely make contact with deceased's family before or after reaping. I still thought that one was stupid and I wasn't certain I'd be able to abide by it. I wondered what kind of punishment I'd incur for breaking it.

It is prohibited to prevent the reap. Only guardian angels have the right to interfere.

A reaper must remain neutral.

It is prohibited to fraternize or engage in ongoing conversations with the client. In other words, don't become their therapist.

On and on the list went. I wondered if Nate had actually memorized all the rules, or if he was just putting on a good show. As I scanned through the rest, I gleaned the general message. Keep a low profile and do the job. How hard could it be? Even though I hated to admit it, I'd always been kind of a rule follower. Being a reaper might be the perfect fit.

Breck scooted into the booth next to me and took a big drink of his soda. Pink tinged his cheeks and sweat coated his forehead.

"You having fun?" I said, clicking off my phone and pocketing it.

He shrugged and toyed with his fries. "It's all right."

"What's wrong?" I scooped a hank of sweaty hair off his forehead. "Is somebody bullying you?"

"No." He bit the end of the French fry and chewed.

Something was definitely wrong. Normally, Breck hog-faced a burger in under a minute, but now he didn't touch it. "You can tell me." I hoped it was something simple, like he'd decided he wanted to be a vampire instead of a ghost. "Come on." I gave him a reassuring smile. "I'm pretty good at solving problems."

His big blue eyes looked up at me. "There's a ghost in the slide tubes and she won't give me back my sock."

My smile tightened. "A ghost?"

Bronte snorted and shook her head. "Moron."

"Hey, stop calling your brother names." I looked back at Breck. "Are you sure it's a ghost and not a kid that stole your sock?"

"Positive. It's an old lady and she's mean."

Solutions and excuses raced through my mind. My son didn't need his sock. We had a hundred singles at home he could wear. And what were the chances of a real live ghost haunting the McDonald's play tube?

"What are you going to do, Mom?" His eyes stared at me, trusting.

"Yeah, Mom, what are you going to do?" Bronte smirked at me.

"Well…" I gently shoved Breck toward the end of the bench. "I'm getting your sock back." I narrowed my gaze at Bronte. "That's what I'm going to do."

My son let me out and I wove my way through the bevy of children and tables and stopped at the end of a long green slide. Every few seconds a kid shot to the bottom and jumped off to circle back for another go, sometimes turning and crawling back up.

Surveying the conglomeration of colorful tubes and nets, I decided that climbing the padded platforms steps would be a lot safer and less humiliating than trying to shove myself up one of the slides. I glanced around. The other parents were busy with their own kids or ignoring the mayhem. I gripped the edge of the platform and slowly worked my way up the play set. Once at the top, I crawled on hands and knees across a netted bridge. Something wet and sticky pressed into my palm. I cringed but continued forward. The smell of dirty feet, chocolate shakes, and pee enveloped me. I tried not the think of the bacteria clinging to every surface I touched.

Note to self: pick up more hand sanitizer.

A small child in an orange sweat suit tried to squeeze past. “Excuse me.”

“Sure thing.” I pressed my body to the side to let him by. When he reached the end of the netted bridge I stopped him. “Hey, have you seen any…um, another lady up here?”

“You mean the ghost lady?”

My eyes rounded and I nodded. “Yeah, the ghost lady.”

“She hangs out next to the yellow slide.” With that the kid scurried away.

I hesitated. If there really was a ghost living in the play set, she wasn't my charge. I pulled out my phone and tapped the appointment app. The screen was empty. Maybe I should leave well enough alone. I could always buy Breck more socks. Unfortunately, curiosity was one of my worst vices.

At the juncture where the net bridge ended, I stopped. Taking a deep breath, I poked my head around the corner. Yep, she was there, all translucent and ghost like. My heart jumped to my throat. I didn't think I'd ever get used to seeing spirits. It's one thing to catch a glimpse in my periphery. Staring at one full on was intimidating in an *I don't know nothin' about reapin' no spirits* way.

"I'm not leaving, so don't waste your time trying to convince me," the ghost said.

I glanced around, but nobody else was there. "Are you talking to me?"

"Who else would I be talking to? Came to try to get me to cross over, right?" She lifted a spectral cigarette to her lips, took a drag so long my lungs hurt, and then blew it out. "Like I told the first guy. I'm not going."

Her words sort of registered but my attention was fixed on her cigarette. I quit smoking two years ago but sometimes the craving still hit. I scooted farther into the padded area, trying to maneuver myself into the line of her ghost smoke, hoping for a hit. I settled against the netted wall across from her and inhaled. The smell was faint, and not as satisfying as I'd hoped for.

"How do you know I'm a reaper?" I started to cross my legs but they still hurt. Instead I stretched them out and crossed my ankles. "Maybe I'm just a mom, who can see ghosts."

"Right." She snorted and held out her hand, indicating the area we sat in. "Because there are so many parents up here."

She had me on that one. Unless a child was hurt, scared, or physically stuck, no parent would dare enter the germ-pool. And even that was questionable, especially if there was an older sibling to send into the tubes to retrieve the child.

"Okay, so I'm a reaper." I pointed to Breck's sock. The end poked out from under her butt. "I wouldn't have bothered you if you hadn't scared my son and refused to give him his sock."

She harrumphed and took another drag.

"So, why are you up here…?" I waited for her name.

"Lily."

"Lily. Is this where you died?" I couldn't imagine someone wanting to spend eternity in a fast food play set.

"No, I died in the hospital. Lung cancer." She

squashed the cigarette onto the mat and after a few seconds it disappeared. "But this is where my daughter comes with my grandkids."

"I'm sorry." And I really was. Missing family must have been the number one cause for hauntings. I didn't have any solid stats, but I was pretty sure I was right. "I bet it's difficult knowing you won't see your grandchildren grow up."

Her face scrunched. "I couldn't give a good gosh darn about my grandkids. They're monsters. Their parents spoil those brats something awful."

Taken aback by the vehemence in her response, I blinked a few times and nodded. "Okay, then I don't get it. Why here?"

"I need to get a message to my daughter."

The clang of warning bells erupted in my head. Rule number one— *It is prohibited to purposely make contact with deceased's family before or after reaping.* It would have been better to say I was sorry and I couldn't help her. Damn my curiosity. "What kind of message?"

The ghost's gaze shifted to me. She stared for a few seconds before saying, "My good-for-nothing son-in-law, Tony, is cheating on my daughter with her best friend."

I gasped. "That bastard."

"That isn't the half of it. Maryanne is pregnant with

his kid."

I sat forward. "Maryanne is the best friend?"

"Yep, and the skank keeps pretending to be my daughter's bestie. Makes me mad enough to possess her."

"What a bitch." I leaned back, completely incensed by the situation. "Your poor daughter."

"She's a good person and doesn't deserve this." The ghost held my stare. "So…"

Don't become the spirit's therapist. Just broke that rule. "I don't know. Can I be honest, Lily. I've only been doing this job for about a week, and passing a message onto family members is a major no-no in the rule book."

"Send her an anonymous letter." The ghost held out her translucent hands. "Who would know?"

I cocked a brow at her. "You do realize who I work for, right."

"Well, maybe if you're casual about it. Tuck it in with your bills and letters, they—" She pointed upward. "Won't notice."

I shouldn't. I mean, I really shouldn't even entertain the idea of getting involved. Delivering the message was not worth the trouble I'd get into.

Suddenly Lily's eyes widened. Scooting onto all fours, she crawled to the edge of the platform to look through the net. "They're here." She pointed to the group of people walking into the play area. “Oh, that whore of a friend is with them.”

I scrambled to join her. Side-by-side, we watched the group claim a table near the door. It wasn’t hard to tell who Lily’s daughter was. Small and blonde like her mother, she appeared haggard and beaten down. The friend, on the other hand, had a rosy glow, and there was no mistaking the furtive glances she tossed in Tony’s direction.

“Okay, I’ll do it.” The words popped out before I could stop myself. I sat back on my heels. “But you have to promise to cross over when it’s done.”

Lily smiled and held up her hand. “Scout’s honor. So, what are you going to do?”

I took a deep breath and exhaled. “Watch and enjoy.” I scooted toward the yellow tube. “Meet me in the parking lot after I leave.”

She nodded.

I crawled across the platform, grabbed Breck’s sock, and sent myself down the yellow tube slide. Standing, I dusted myself off and glanced up. Lily was still pressed against the net, watching me. Instead of heading straight back to my kids, I skirted the center tables and walked toward Lily’s daughter.

I was never much of an actress, so I drew my motivation from experience. Believing Jeff had been cheating on me was a hurt that cut into my soul, but I would have wanted to know. Still, I hated that I was about to open a can of hurt for Lily's daughter.

As I passed their table, I casually glanced over. Pasting on a big smile, I stopped. "Hey, sorry to bother you." I pointed to Maryanne. "But I recognized you two from the doctor's office, and just wanted to say congratulations on the baby."

The blood drained from Maryanne's face and her eyes cut to Lily's daughter. "I don't know what you're talking about."

"You and your husband." I pointed at Tony. "The girls at the doctor's office and I were talking about how cute you two were together."

Lily's daughter leaned forward on her arm, resting them on the table. "That's *my* husband."

I let my eyes go wide. "But, you and he—" I didn't finish my sentence. If Lily's daughter were smart she'd put two and two together. "Okay, well, sorry."

With that I continued to my table. Bryce had joined Bronte and Breck. They'd polished off most of their meals and would be ready to go in another five minutes. "I've got to make a call." I tossed Breck's sock to him and then grabbed my purse from the corner of the booth. "I'll be right back."

"Did you see her, Mom?" Breck shoved his foot into the hole and pulled on his sock. "Did you see the ghost?"

I repressed the urge to look in Lily's direction. "Nope, just your sock." I ruffled his hair. "It probably stunk so bad she didn't want to keep it." He smiled and went back to eating his fries. "Okay, finish up and I'll be back in a second."

As I passed the table where Lily's family sat, I heard their heated conversation. I'd placed the spark of doubt and her daughter was running with it. Pushing open the glass door, I pulled out my phone and walked outside to wait for Lily. I fingered the raven charm hanging around my neck. I'd put it on when I got home and vowed to never take it off. Hopefully it would protect me from Hal's allure.

The temperature had dropped several degrees over the past half hour. I zipped my coat all the way up and shoved my free hand into my pocket. A squawk sounded above me and I glanced up to see Fletcher perched on the light pole. Relief washed through me. Hopefully, the bird's presence meant this would be a smooth transaction.

Lily appeared beside me, a big grin on her face. "That did it." She held out her hand. "Thanks."

I reached out and shook her hand, but didn't let go. "You're welcome. I'm glad I could help—even if I do get in trouble."

"What are they going to do? Fire you?" Lily said.

I thought about that for a second. "Good point. I don't really know." I shrugged. "So, are you ready?"

A heavy sigh heaved from the ghost. "Ready as I'll ever be."

"I want to warn you, my porter is a little unorthodox, but don't be scared. He'll get you to where you need to be."

A mischievous gapped grin spread across her face. "Sounds interesting."

I turned my back to the restaurant and lifted the phone to my ear, pretending to be taking a call. Still holding onto Lily, I called, "Hal Lee Lewya."

Fletcher squawked and flapped his wings. This time I didn't have to wait. The thin pink line of light formed and the elevator door slid open. I glanced at Lily, gaging her reaction.

Her grin rounded to an astonished O. "What in the name of God's green Earth is that?"

I had to admit, Hal had outdone himself. Dressed in a bright red, satin pants and shirt, he glimmered in the fading sunlight. "Well, Lily, that is Hal Lee Lewya."

"He looks more like a Las Vegas pimp."

"Lisa." His voice caressed me as it had at GRS, but the effect was very different. There was no urge to go to him. "I didn't realize we had a client."

"We didn't, but now we do." I took two steps forward and stopped, making sure to stay out of his range. "Lily needs to cross." I pinned him with a glower. "You'll make sure she gets to where she's supposed to be, right?"

"Of course." He held out his hand. "But what do you say to a little fun first, Lily?"

"Uh uh." I wagged an index finger in his direction. "No deviations. Just straight to her check-in point, or whatever you call it."

Hal's lower lip rolled into a pout. "Perhaps just the first circle of Hell—"

"No." I cut him off. "No circles."

"Then maybe Lily would like to see the river Styx."

Actually, *I* wouldn't have minded seeing the river Styx. I open my mouth to reply, but Lily beat me to it.

"Maybe a few detours wouldn't be so bad." She smiled at Hal. "I mean, it's not like I'm on a deadline, right?"

I didn't know if she was or not, but I could see I wasn't going to sway these two. "So help me, Hal, if you do anything—"

"Yes, I know, you'll report me." He wiggled his fingers in Lily's direction. "She'll be fine."

Even if she wasn't, what could I do? Take her to GRS and put her in Purgatory? But then they'd know I broke the message to loved ones rule. Yeah, I was completely covering my own ass.

"All right, I'm going to trust you, Hal." Of course I didn't. "Our relationship is new, and I want to start off on the right foot." He lifted a brow, and I got the distinct impression he was more entertained than moved by my 'go team' speech. So I changed tactics. "You scratch my back and I'll scratch yours—if you catch my meaning."

His expression morphed into a slightly evil smile. "Perfectly, Lisa Carron."

With nothing further to say, I released Lily's hand. She drifted to Hal and into the elevator. "Bye, Lily." I waved. "Have a good afterlife."

"You can count on it." She ran her hand down Hal's arm. "I need a set of these fancy pajamas."

"Your wish is my command, Miss Lily."

With that, the elevator door closed and folded into a thin beam of light before vanishing. I lowered my phone and looked up at Fletcher. I was fairly certain the bird was my familiar and had kept Hal's mojo and bay. "Thanks."

The raven flapped his wings and launched into the sky. I took a deep breath and released it, hoping I hadn't just gotten myself in a heap of trouble.

CHAPTER FOURTEEN

Halloween day worked out better than I could have planned. My mother picked up the boys in the morning so they could enjoy an entire day of Halloween festivities. Bronte left for Fang's house around two o'clock. It seemed that once she'd accepted she couldn't go to the party, Fang and a group of girls had decided to opt out and have a sleepover instead. I will admit to feeling a bit smug in my efforts to protect our youth. The other parents could thank me later.

With the kids gone, I was free to spend the day preparing for my busy night. It took several rounds of trying on clothes before I settled on an appropriate reaping outfit. For me it was all about the clothes. Before I took up any sport or activity I had to have the proper attire. Otherwise, I felt like I wasn't fully committed. Lucky for me, my wardrobe was reaper ready.

Temperatures so far had been colder than normal and

I figured tonight wouldn't be any different. After a lot of kicking, punching, and standing outside to see if the clothes were warm enough, I settled on a black turtleneck sweater and black polar fleece pants. I pilfered a black stocking cap and gloves from our winter clothes bin, and pulled out my black shearling lined boots.

The outfit was perfect, but when I stood in front of the mirror assessing myself, I realized I wanted an even bigger change. I was a reaper now, not just a mom who fell into the position. I'd embraced it, well—kind of, and despite Nate's skepticism, I'd passed all the tests. I'd even reaped Lily without any help.

After pulling out my phone, I dialed Vella.

"Vella's Star Power Salon, how may I help you?"

"I'm ready," I said.

Silence stretched on the other end of the phone, until she finally said, "Platinum and sassy?"

"Bring it on!" I clicked off the phone and set it on the dresser. If I knew my friend, she'd close up shop and be at my house in fifteen minutes. She'd been chomping at the bit to get ahold of my hair for years. Telling her to bring it on was like waving crack in front of an addict. And I had to admit, for the first time I wasn't afraid of change. I wanted different. I needed to let go of the old me and embrace my reaper, and Vella was the gal for the task.

By the time Nate picked me up that evening, I'd found my reaper mojo. My hair was short and spikey, except for the two thin pieces she'd left at the sides, and my new platinum color glimmered like a pearl in the bathroom light. I hated to wear a hat but necessity demanded it. Besides, the little sprigs of blond peeking out looked kind of hot. I felt like a character in a spy movie.

One look from Nate told me I'd made the right choice. "You look…great."

"Thanks." I climbed into the passenger side of the Suburban. "I really needed a change."

He stared at me a few seconds and then shifted into reverse. "You ready for tonight?"

"As ready as I'll ever be." I clicked my seatbelt. "Where are we going?"

"Out to one of the lakes in Wasilla." He pushed the gear into drive. "Did you get the assignment on your phone?"

"Yeah, a Nuk Fulsom? But I didn't see any details on how he's going to die."

"There's a details tab in the corner. It drops down and give you more information."

I didn't feel like digging my phone out of my pocket and trying to read as we drove. "So what are the details?"

"Headless Horseman," he said.

"Excuse me?"

He smirked. "Or, I should say Headless snow machiner."

People in the lower forty-eight call them snowmobiles. Up here we call them snow machines. I always figured it was a location thing, like pop versus soda. I scowled at Nate. "That sounds gross."

"Not as bad as it sounds. Some guys are trying to cross thin ice with pumpkins on their heads."

My brows lifted. "That is one of the stupidest things I've ever heard."

"Yep." He glanced at me and then to the road again. "Those are your clients."

The little bit of ego boost I'd gained from reaping Lily evaporated. I had a feeling the Lily-like reaps would be few, and pumpkin-wearing ignoramuses would be numerous. Thankfully, Nate didn't jab with any more verbal barbs.

The drive took an hour. A veil of snow lay in a white sheet across the ground and the full moon made it sparkle like blue diamonds. Nate pulled onto the narrow road and shut off the lights. With only the moon to see by, he inched down the road until reaching the end. Four other cars were parked there, and he pulled alongside the last one on the left and shut off the engine.

From where we sat we had a perfect view of the men

on the lake. The whine of the snow machine pierced the night as one of the guys took off across the ice, pumpkin firmly resting over his head. I unhooked my seatbelt and sat forward. The breath stuck in my throat as I watched him shoot across the lake. Would this be the guy I'd have to reap?

Until now I never thought much about seeing the death take place. I only concentrated on getting the soul. "How did you say this guy dies?"

"The ice breaks."

My head snapped in Nate's direction. "Then how am I supposed to get to him?"

"His soul will be on the ice, watching his friends."

My gaze swung back to the group of guys. "How can you be sure?"

"They always linger. Either because they don't know they're dead, or they want to make sure somebody finds their body."

"I hope you're right."

We watched the antics for another fifteen minutes. A lot of heavy stuff rolled through me. As a mother, I wanted to march out there and tell them what idiots they were and to stop it before somebody got killed. As a reaper, I wanted to get the job over with and go home. As a human it was uncanny to watch an individual's life count down, while they had no idea. The knowledge was a gift and a curse. It made me feel powerful, and yet insignificant against death's force. I'd fallen into this job, and had accepted it begrudgingly. Realizing the scope of my obligations humbled me.

The steady whine of the snow machine motor broke, drawing my attention back to the lake. Just like Nate said, the ice cracked, giving way. One second Nuk Fulsom was there and the next he was gone. Even though I knew it was coming, having it actually happen was still a shock. I gasped and slapped my hands over my mouth. After few seconds I covered my eyes, trying not to cry.

"You okay, Carron?"

I nodded but didn't reply, not trusting my voice. Screams from the other guys filtered through our closed windows. My stomach roiled and threatened to revolt and took several deep breaths to calm my nausea. Finally I looked up again.

"It's about time." Nate paused. "You ready?"

I saw Nuk's glimmering spirit standing beside his friends. "How do we do this?"

"I'll divert the guys and help them retrieve Nuk's body. You get ahold of his spirit and lead it off the thin ice."

"Be careful." Fear for Nate's safety coursed through me. "You're not one of my reaps tonight are you?"

"No." He shook his head and smiled. "But thanks for

worrying."

"Okay." I held up my gloves. "Can I wear these?"

"Yep. Clothing doesn't interfere."

I nodded and slipped them on. When I was finished, I pulled on the door handle. "I'm ready."

We exited the Suburban and made our way down the slope to the lake. Nate headed for the guys and I cut a path to Nuk. He continued to stare at his friends, not noticing me. "Nuk."

He didn't move.

"Nuk," I said again.

Still the guy didn't respond.

"Nuk!"

"What?"

It wasn't the ghost who answered. I spun to face a very wet, very much alive man. "You're Nuk?"

He sniffed and wiped his arm across his eyes. "Yeah."

"Who broke through?" I was completely confused since the dead guy was still alive, and now I didn't have any idea who I was supposed to reap.

"Eddie, my friend." Nuk glanced back at the open water.

"Did you—" I scrambled for something to say. "Did you call 911?"

"Yeah, they're on their way." He moved toward the group.

I turned to the ghost. "Eddie?"

"Yeah." He sidled up beside me, his hands shoved in his coat pocket. "Am I dead?"

"Uh, yes—yes you are. Sorry."

He shrugged. "At least my death was awesome."

I grunted. "Seriously? You think falling through thin ice with a pumpkin on your head constitutes an awesome death?"

"Hell yeah." He grinned at me. "You know what would have been really cool?" He didn't wait for my reply. "If we would have lit the pumpkins on fire like the real Headless Horseman."

Okay, I wasn't going to impart any afterlife-changing pearls of wisdom, so I pushed forward with the agenda. "Eddie, you need to cross over and I need to get home to hand out Halloween candy." I took a step toward him. "Would that be all right?"

His brow furrowed. "Are you telling me you're the grim reaper?"

I held out my arms. "In the flesh."

"You're hot."

"Really?" I asked, surprised by his compliment.

"Hell yeah. I would have done this a lot sooner if I'd

known hot babes were angels of death."

Idiot. "Thanks." I took him by the arm and led him to the lake's edge. "I like you, Eddie."

He edge closer to me, pressing his cold ghostly body into mine, literally. I jumped back. "Not like that." A shiver ran the entire length of my spine. "Now stay." I grabbed his arm again. "I'm going to pass you off to my porter and I promise he'll show you a good time. Okay?"

Eddie nodded, a stupid grin plastered on his face. "Awesome."

"Yes, it's awesomely awesome." I tilted my chin up. "Hal."

Instantly the thin line of light appeared. One thing about Hal, he was prompt. The door slid open and he stood in a floor-length, white fur coat.

"Whoa," Eddie said.

"Indeed," I replied. "Now that's awesome, right?"

"Dude, I love the threads."

"A man of great taste," Hal said. His yellow gaze skated to me. "Lisa, you bring me the most entertaining clients."

"I trust Lily got where she needed to be?" I asked.

"Delivered to the Pearly Gates early this morning." His gold tooth winked at me. "That is, after a turn around the first circle of Hell."

"I said no tours."

"She asked to go, and loved it." He waved a silver cane in my direction. "The first circle is nothing more than a bunch of whining pagans. Now the third circle—" Hal looked at Eddie. "I think you'd enjoy that. Sex twenty-four-seven."

Eddie looked at me. "Thanks for setting this up. It's even better than I imagined."

"I didn't arrange this." I glared at Hal. "What do you get, a cut on how many souls you lure into Hell?"

"Lisa, when will you learn, I simply want to have fun?" He waved Eddie to him. "And this young man not only likes my clothing, but seems ready for a little excitement as well."

I glared at both of them and finally let go of the ghost's arm. "Fine, but don't come crying to me if you get in trouble—either of you."

"Let your conscience be clear, sweet Lisa."

"And don't call me that."

Eddie moved into the elevator and turned to face me. As the doors closed he grinned and waved. "See you on the other side."

"I certainly hope not," I mumbled.

As the portal disappeared, my phone erupted in my pocket. I fumbled with the zipper and finally pulled it free. It was my mother.

“Hi, Mom, is everything all right?” Icy wind whipped around me, but it wasn’t as chilling as my mother’s words.

“Bronte’s been in a car accident.”

CHAPTER FIFTEEN

"I'm on my way." My mind turned to white-hot panic. "Nate, we've got to go!"

"What's going on?"

I started running across the snow-covered ground. "My daughter's been in a car accident."

The crunch of footsteps sounded behind me, letting me know Nate was close on my heels. Tears stung my eyes and streamed down my cheeks, burning in the cold. A huge lump formed in my throat. As I barreled up the snowy bank to Nate's Suburban, I could hardly breathe. Was Bronte badly hurt—or worse?

Once at the truck I reached for the handle. My fingers gripped the door but began to shake. Shivers wracked my body, not from the cold, but from having to relive another possible death. The same crippling emotions I experienced the night Jeff died swamped me. Shallow sobs huffed from me as I wrestled with the door handle. *Not my baby. Anybody but my kids.*

Nate's strong hands gripped my shoulder and moved me away from the door. I fought against him. "I need to get to her."

"I know." He blocked me and opened the door. "I'll drive you to the hospital."

We stared at each other for a few seconds while my brain processed what he said. Finally, I nodded and crawled into the passenger seat, my body trembling.

Nate climbed into the driver's seat. "Put on your seatbelt." I glared at him. "The roads are slippery, Lisa. Bronte needs you safe. Buckle up."

Somehow his terse words penetrated my panic. I yanked the strap around me and jammed it into the buckle. "Drive."

He slammed the Suburban into gear. The vehicle fishtailed, but he easily maintained control. We drove in silence all the way back to Anchorage, allowing every imaginable scenario to pummel my mind. What would I find once we reached the hospital? All my mother had said was there had been a car accident and Bronte was involved. I hadn't heard anything after that.

I wiped the sleeve of my jacket across my eyes. Pulling myself out of the grief after Jeff's death had been hard enough. I wasn't sure I'd be so lucky if Bronte was dead.

Dead, like the young man I'd just reaped. I closed my eyes and sent up a silent prayer. "Please, not my daughter."

But what if she had been killed? Would the task to reap her fall to me? When Vella had asked if I would have wanted to help my husband pass when he died I'd said no. At the time I'd meant it. Now, facing that very situation, I knew I'd give anything to see and talk to Bronte one last time.

The miles flew by in a blur, but it seemed to take forever to get to the hospital. Finally, Nate pulled up to the emergency entrance. "Go on. I'll park and find you."

Not waiting for the Suburban to stop, I flung the door open and raced through the automatic doors, skidding to a stop in front of the reception desk. "I'm Lisa Carron. My daughter was brought in. She was in a car accident."

Maybe it was the panic in my voice, or the crazed mother-on-the-edge look on my face, but the woman snatched a visitor pass from the wall and came out of her office. "I'll escort you back. Here, put this on." She gave a single wave to the security guard in the booth directly across from her cubicle. "Lisa Carron."

He nodded.

The woman pressed a large round button on the wall. With agonizing slowness the double doors opened. I shifted my weight from foot to foot, barely able to control the urge to push past her. Not that I'd know where to go. I'd probably start shouting for Bronte, get arrested, or at the very least, medicated. So I waited.

The only person at the desk was a young, tall male nurse. He glanced up as we approached.

"Michael, this is Lisa Carron. Her daughter is one of the kids in the car accident." The receptionist turned and faced me. "He'll take care of you."

"Thank you," was all I could manage.

As she passed me, she placed a hand on my shoulder, sending a wave of warmth through my body. I glanced at her hand, and then to her face. She smiled and I recognized her as one of the gifted. Not a grim reaper, but perhaps a wannabe or even a guardian angel. I nodded and returned my attention to Michael.

"Is my daughter…" My voice cracked. "Is my daughter alive?"

He looked up from the chart. "Yes, a broken arm, but nothing worse."

Tension rushed from my muscles, deflating me like a balloon. At that same moment Nate arrived. I turned and buried my face in his jacket, and his arms went around me without hesitation. For once I was grateful for his solid chest and strength.

After another minute of sobbing into his coat, I

sniffed and stepped away. “Are the other kids okay?”

I’d just assumed everybody in the car had cuts and bruises but nothing worse.

The nurse shook his head and lowered his voice. “The driver was dead on arrival.”

His words hit me like a slap. “Oh my God.” My hand flew to my mouth. “Who was it?”

Michael flipped through the pages on a clipboard. “Kelly Huff.” He looked at me. “Her parents just arrived.”

Nausea rolled through my body. I bent, bracing my hands on my knees and tried to get a breath. Nate rubbed my back, but didn’t say anything. The anger over Bronte disobeying me was dwarfed by the fact that even though she’d narrowly escaped being killed, Kelly Huff had not. I stood and wrapped my arms around my torso. “Can I see my daughter, please?”

“Of course.”

We followed Michael along the corridor, passing several curtained off rooms. We stopped half way down the hallway. Movement drew my attention toward the end. Three people exited a room. A knot formed in my throat when the woman turned to one of the men and buried her face in his coat. The other person, obviously a doctor from the way he was dressed, spoke softly and then left the two alone.

“Kelly’s parents.” My voice cracked.

I wanted to go to them, offer my condolences, but the action felt too intrusive. What could I possibly say? No parent should outlive their child—ever. And the fact that mine was still alive suddenly seemed unfair somehow.

Nate put his hand and on my back and guided me into the room. At first I was resistant but then I saw Bronte lying in the bed, her face covered with bruises and cuts, her arm in a sling. I practically ran to her. She turned her head and looked at me, tears streaming down her face. At that moment, my only thought was of comforting her. I wrapped my arms around her and pulled her gently to me, careful not to hurt her.

She turned her face toward my neck. "I'm sorry, Mom."

"Me too, baby." I kissed the top of her head, letting my lips linger in her hair. "Me too."

"The doctor will be with you in a few minutes," Michael said, and slipped out of the room.

From the doorway Nate said, "I'll be right back."

I turned my head, still resting my cheek against Bronte's head. "Where are you going?"

"I need to check on a few things." He tugged the curtain closed, leaving Bronte and me alone.

It didn't take super-duper reaper intuition to know he'd gone to reap Kelly Huff. A chill ran up my spine, and I closed my eyes. Some days I really hated this job.

Though it took all my willpower, I unwound my arms from Bronte, and pulled the chair in the corner up to the side of the bed. I claimed her hand, needing to touch her. We sat in silence until her tears finally dried. Now that some of the shock had worn off, questions bubbled inside me, but I didn't ask them, not wanting to traumatize my daughter any more than she had been tonight.

After another few minutes she said, "I'm sorry I disobeyed you, Mom. I promise to never do it again."

A humorless laugh hiccupped from me. "If only that were true." I chanced a little parenting. "Why did you do it?"

She shrugged and winced. "It sounds lame, but Fang begged me to go. You may have noticed that me and my friends aren't actually that popular." She hesitated. "I knew Kelly was just using us to get to William, so I decided to use her to get into the in crowd."

"I didn't think you cared about popularity contests?" It seemed she wasn't the only one learning a lesson tonight.

Since the day she was born, Bronte had had her own style. She never seemed to care about what was cool. At least I hadn't thought so. I was wrong.

"I never did—don't really, but Fang does. She said if I was a good friend I'd suffer through the night."

"Even though I said no?"

Bronte nodded.

"Still, you made the decision. You have to take responsibility for that."

"I know, and I won't argue with whatever punishment you give me." She let her head fall back and rest against her pillow. "Maybe you could ground me for a year so I don't have to see anybody."

"A whole year? Don't you think we've already had a year of punishment?"

Her gaze captured mine. Tears puddled, magnifying her blue eyes. "All I could think about was what you were going to do when you heard I'd been in a car accident. You know, after Dad and all."

I swallowed hard. "I won't lie, Bronte, that was one of the worst moments of my life." A single tear spilled down her cheek, but I wiped it away with my thumb. "And hearing that you were alive was one of the best."

"So what now?"

"We go on from here." I leaned forward and swiped a matted chunk of hair from her face. "Live our lives. That's the best we can do."

Before she could reply the curtain whipped open. "Bronte." My mother sailed into the room and threw herself at her granddaughter. "We thought you were dead."

"Grandma, I can't breathe," Bronte's muffled voice

emanated from my mother's armpit.

I looked at my dad. For the first time that I could remember, genuine emotion played across his face. His pale skin accentuated his wide-eyed stare, as if staring at a ghost. "Dad, you okay?"

His gaze slid to me. "Yeah." His voice was raspy and I had the urge to get up and hug him, but I didn't. If my dad started to cry, I would lose it completely.

"Where are the boys?"

"We left them with Vella," my mother said. "She wants you to call her as soon as you get a chance."

I'd have to do something nice for her. Not having to worry about the boys was worth two bottles of wine and several hours of listening to stories about her crazy family.

Seeing Nate lingering just outside the door, I stood and patted my mom's back. "I'll be right back." On my way out I pulled the curtain closed again. "Well?" I whispered at Nate.

"Well what?"

I gripped his wrist and pulled him away from Bronte's room. "Kelly Huff, did you reap her."

"No."

I let go of his arm. "Why not? I thought that's where you went."

He glanced down the hall, and then back to me. "I did

but she wasn't there."

I narrowed my gaze. "What do you mean she wasn't there?"

"Somebody reaped her already."

"Are you sure?"

He sneered at me. "I think I know when there's no soul."

"Sorry. It's just weird, is all." I paced a few steps. "That *is* weird, right?"

"Weird but not impossible. Somebody might have been in the area. I don't know."

"Is there any way to find out who?"

Nate stared at me for a few seconds. "It doesn't matter, Lisa. Kelly is gone. Job done."

"But—"

"But nothing." He took my hand and led me back to Bronte's room. "You need to focus on your family right now. Not worry about who—," his voice dropped to a whisper, "finished the job."

I stopped at the entrance. Nate let go of my hand, but didn't go into the room. He was right. Bronte needed me, but more than that, I needed her, and my boys. "Thanks for being there tonight. I don't know what I would have done without you."

His lips spread into a tight smile. "Don't mention it,

Carron. That's what partners do for each other—right?"

Had he just called me his partner? Without coercion? Without threat of death? Not wanting to spoil our one, fragile moment with sarcasm, I nodded. "Yeah, they do."

A slight blush crept across his cheeks. He shifted uncomfortably and then flicked his head toward the exit. "I'm gonna hit the road." He shoved his hands in his front pockets. "This seems like a family affair."

"Okay, thanks."

He turned to leave but stopped. "Take a few days off. I'll cover your assignments," he said over his shoulder, not looking at me.

I didn't reply and he didn't seem to expect one. His step never slowing, he strode down the hall. I watched until he turned the corner. Who knew Nate Cramer, reaper extraordinaire, had a heart? I hadn't, but it wasn't a mistake I'd make again. And as far as Kelly Huff's spirit, that was another issue. Maybe one day we'd discover who reaped her, but for now I wanted to forget about everything except taking care of my daughter.

It seemed death would be my constant companion from now on, and I could either be consumed by it or own it. I decided to own it. Suck it, Death! There's a new reaper in town.

Styx & Stoned

Book 2 of the Grim Reality Series

Chapter One

Las Vegas! All expenses paid!

Normally, a trip like that would be a dream come true for an overworked, widowed, mother of three. Here's the thing, though; situations rarely worked out as I imagined. And usually not in my favor. So, when my boss, Constantine, offered—well, not actually offered…more like handed me—the plane ticket to Vegas and told me in no uncertain terms I'd be attending the GRS annual convention, I was instantly suspicious.

GRS stands for Grim Reaper Services, of which I, Lisa Carron, am their newest grim reaper. And sadly, the least adept. I was getting better, but I'd been a reaper for less than a year and had nowhere near the skills my partner Nate possessed.

And don't get me started about Constantine. He's our crazy hot Alaskan leader, but I still hadn't decided if he was human. Actually, I'm scared to be alone with him. Not in a hockey-mask-psycho-killer way. More like, if I was ever pressed up against his body, I wasn't sure I'd be able to stop my hands from roving to his forbidden zones. I just couldn't be trusted in a situation like that.

So here I was in sunny Las Vegas, seven kid-free days, and none of it costing me a dime. I should have been giddy, spinning around the baggage claim area like Maria in The Sound of Music. But, like I said, circumstances were never what they seemed. I couldn't shake the feeling that this week had nothing to do with Lisa time and everything to do with other people's agendas. Even so, I planned to take advantage of the numerous luxuries the hotel spa had to offer.

The airport's electronic doors slid open and the hot desert air enveloped me. Exhaust clawed at my throat. I gasped and squinted against the blinding Vegas sun. How did people live in this heat? The better question might be, why? Sixteen degrees and accumulating darkness—that's what I'd left behind in Anchorage. Las Vegas was like anti-Alaska.

I hauled my ancient, massive suitcase toward the line of taxicabs, beads of sweat instantly forming across the bridge of my nose and forehead. The material of my long-sleeved T-shirt clung like a second skin, and the sun reflecting off the pavement, plus all the altitude changes, made my head throb. My flight had left Anchorage at midnight and I'd spent several hours wandering around the Seattle airport, waiting for the tram to start up so I could get to my concourse. Tired didn't describe my current condition.

Now I understood why people huddled like vampires inside the dark, cool casinos. Sit at a slot machine receiving free drinks, or venture into the blistering heat to stare at Hoover Dam. I know what my choice would be.

"Cab?" A valet waved me over and pointed at the first cab in the long line waiting at the curb. His tone was all business. "Right here."

I lopped toward him, but he'd already focused on the person behind me, and was moving to the next cab. I shoved my bag toward the cab driver. "The Venetian, please."

"Excellent." He grinned, his white teeth gleaming against his dark skin. "Please, get in and enjoy the air-conditioned comfort of my cab."

His thick Indian accent and invitation made him sound like a commercial for the cab company. While he manhandled my suitcase toward the trunk of the car, I climbed into the back seat. A sigh hissed from me when the cool air hit my skin. I tossed my jacket and purse next to me and leaned my head against the back of the seat. My eyes drifted closed. Several thumps vibrated against the back seat, sending a pang of embarrassment through me. No matter how many times I'd packed and unpacked to thin out what I'd need, I still ended up with far more clothes than I could possibly wear in a week.

I lifted my head and opened my eyes, squinting against the sun streaming through the front window. For the first time I noticed the older man sitting in the front passenger seat. "Oh, hello." He didn't respond. Maybe he didn't speak or understand

English. Now committed to the acknowledgement, I repeated my greeting. "Hi."

His head snapped around, his eyes widening. "Are you talking to me?"

"Yes, I am." Mystery solved about not understanding English. I smiled. "You're smart to stay in the car. That heat is killer."

"Very funny," he said, glaring. Then he shifted to face me.

"Crap." The downside of being a grim reaper was that I was always on the job. The right side of the man's head wavered like one of those heat mirages on the road. "You're dead." I scowled at him. "Aren't you?"

"Yes, I am." His lips pursed for a second, looking dubious. "How can you see me?"

"Just one of the perks of my job." The trunk slammed, making me jump. Conversing with ghost tended to be off-putting to those who couldn't see them. I rushed on. "I'm a grim reaper. If you'd like to cross over, I can help you with that when I get to the hotel."

The cab door opened and the driver slid in, cutting off my conversation with the spirit. "Venetian, you said?"

"Yes please…" My gaze cut from the rear view mirror to the identification card fixed to the dash. "Rashid."

"Yes, very good."

"Cross over?" The spirit launched into a tirade as the cab

pulled away. "And leave this bonehead to run my company into the ground? No thank you."

Family drama, so not what I needed right now. After a minute of trying to ignore the ranting specter, I realized the only way to shut him up was to talk over him. "Rashid, does it always get this hot in Vegas?"

"Oh, yes." The cabbie smiled into the rear view mirror. "But you're in luck—it's not supposed to get above ninety this week."

"That's lucky?"

His white-toothed smile reflected back at me, his head nodding vigorously.

I groaned. "How can you stand it?"

"I'm from India." His gaze darted from the road to the mirror, and then back again. "My parents moved us here when I was twelve and opened the taxi business. When my father passed away a year ago, I took over." His smile widened. "Las Vegas is my home now. I love it here, heat and all."

"And if you spent less time enjoying the sights and more time working—" the ghost grumbled.

Again, I cut the spirit off before he hurled himself into another lecture that only I'd be privy to. "I think it's wonderful you love where you live." Glancing at the ghost, I added, "I'm sorry about your father's passing."

"Thank you. It was a great loss for the family," Rashid said.

"Of course it was." His father straightened, jutting his chin upward and crossing his arms over his chest. "I held this family together. Obviously, the entire household is lost without my guidance."

"But…" Rashid caught my eye in the mirror again and grimaced. "To be honest, he was a miserable man."

"Miserable?" The spirit's head whipped toward his son.

I sunk deeper into the seat, bracing myself for the wave of anger I knew would hit me in a few seconds.

"If working eighty hours a week to put food on the table for my family made me miserable, then I'm guilty." Like a blast of Vegas heat, the ghost's resentment pounded me—yet another the neat side effects of being a grim reaper.

"He was never happy with anybody or anything," the cabbie continued.

"What was there to be happy about? You're all a bunch of boneheads. Never listened to anything I said."

"On and on he'd rail about how we didn't appreciate what he'd built for us," Rashid said.

"Yes, I'm getting that," I mumbled to myself.

"Because you didn't." His father waved his hands in the air. "I'd barely been dead a month before this one—" He jabbed a finger at his son. "—started taking Sundays off. No respect. No respect!"

"Call me optimistic, but I like to think he's happy and in a much better place now."

Instead of the sarcastic snort I wanted to make, I pressed my lips together and nodded, giving him my best empathetic expression. "I'm sure you're right."

"Lazy dogs, every one of them." The ghost glared out the front window. "Your mother and I should have never reproduced."

"I'm certain he's exactly where he wants to be," I replied. That wasn't a lie, just the comforting truth Rashid, and every other person who'd lost a loved one, wanted to hear.

"I loved my father and I miss him, but I don't miss his constant complaining."

"Ungrateful…" The spirit faded, taking his angry mojo with him.

That's one downside of being a grim reaper. People think the ability to see the dead is cool. What they don't realize is that the afterlife isn't all white light and feathers. Sometimes it's just a lot of cranky ghosts that have their ectoplasmic panties in a wad.

Laying my head against the back seat, I let my eyelids drift shut. The driver switched topics and began regaling me with Las Vegas trivia. The combination of the cool air and my exhaustion made concentrating on what he said impossible, and after a few seconds, I dozed off.

When the taxi pulled to a stop in front of the hotel I snapped awake, sitting forward with a jolt. A young man in a gray suit yanked open the door. "Ma'am."

"Oh…yeah." I blinked a couple of times, my lids scraping across my eyeballs. Still trying to get my bearings, I scooped up my purse and jacket, and scooted out of the cab. "Thanks."

Either Las Vegas had denser gravity or my exhaustion was making it difficult to move my legs. Though Rashid had parked under the hotel's covered entrance, out of the sun, it was still hot, and I was anxious to get to my room and crank up the AC.

"You made it." Nate's voice sounded behind me. "I was getting worried."

I pivoted to face my partner and couldn't help scowling a little. He'd arrived the day before and had time to rest. As usual, his sandy-brown hair lay perfectly tousled, looking carefree yet stylish. "Were you worried or irritated?"

"I've checked us in." He smirked, not answering my question, and then handed me a small envelope. "The room number is on the inside of the booklet."

"Great, but…" I glanced at him. "We're not rooming together—right?"

"You wish, Carron."

"You wish I wished, Cramer." Okay, it wasn't the best comeback, but I was tired and either needed alcohol and something covered in cheese, or a bath and twenty-four hours of comatose sleep.

The sound of my suitcase hitting the ground thunked behind the cab, followed by the rattle of its wheels running across the tiled drive. With a pearly white smile in place, Rashid wheeled the bag to me. Before I could fish money out of my purse, Nate handed him a stack of folded bills.

"Thank you, sir." Rashid's smile widened. "You're very generous."

"And thank you for a clean, air-conditioned ride." I said, hooking my hand around the handle of my suitcase. "And information about Las Vegas. Truly enlightening."

"My pleasure." Rashid gave a slight bow and pulled a business card out of his front shirt pocket. "Call me for all your taxi needs—except on Sunday."

Nice. My own personal driver. I had no intention of leaving the casino, but I'd learned long ago my plans and fate usually raced along different tracks, sometimes colliding. I accepted the card. "I certainly will."

"Here, let me get that." Nate took the suitcase from me and wheeled it into the hotel.

My eyes narrowed on his broad back. Something was up. He was being exceptionally considerate and I didn't like it one bit. I strode into the hotel after him, my senses on high alert. Again, lovely cool air greeted me when I entered the lobby. A myriad of dings, rings, and bleeps filtered in from the casino. At the sound of their taunting call my energy rallied. Maybe a few rounds of slots would help me unwind before crashing.

Scanning the grand entrance, my gaze skated over the

opulent décor and landed on the milling crowd. My steps slowed to a stop. "Whoa."

Nate turned to me. "What?"

"Is it just me or are there a ton of ghosts in here?" At least half the people were spirits, floating through the living, talking, and some looking rather lost. Alaska didn't have near this number of spirits. "Is this usual of Vegas?"

"Probably." Nate guided my suitcase toward the elevators. "Don't worry about it now. We need to get to the GRS meet-and-greet."

"No." I groaned, my shoulders slumping as I stomped after him. "I need a shower and sleep."

"Later." He pressed the up arrow. "Put your suitcase in your room and come back to the third floor." His attention zeroed on me. "Attendance is mandatory—especially yours."

A niggle of foreboding surfaced and the hair on the back of my neck stood on end. I cocked my head. "Why especially me?"

The elevator to our right dinged, settled, and the doors slid open. We shifted, staying out of the way to allow the car to empty, and then entered.

When the doors closed, Nate punched the three and twenty-six. Still not looking at me, he said, "There are some people you need to meet."

The elevator lurched and started upward. I gripped the handrail, breathing deeply. Normally, I avoided elevators whenever possible. My induction into reaperhood had involved a convenience store shooting, an angry ghost, and the elevator to Hell. Even though I accepted my fate as a reaper, sometimes I still had problems reconciling the whole other world concept, and elevators seemed to be my trigger.

I focused on Nate and ignored my roiling nerves. He had a way of talking around things and I'd learned direct questions got the best results. "What people?"

"Other GRS personnel."

"Can't I meet them tomorrow?" I watched for any sign that he was keeping something from me. His lips pressed together and for a second his nostrils flared before he schooled his expression again. Bingo. Flaring nostrils were always a dead giveaway. "What aren't you telling me?"

"Nothing." He scowled but didn't meet my eyes. Liar. The elevator hiccupped to a stop on the third floor and the doors glided open. Before exiting he looked at me. "Thirty minutes, Carron, right here."

"Yeah, yeah." I punched the close door button three times, causing Nate to hop over the threshold as the metal slabs slid shut. "Jerk," I said to the empty car.

The elevator spit me out on the twenty-sixth floor. With no small amount of effort, I wrestled my suitcase through the doors that kept trying to close on me, and down the carpeted hall. Finally, I found my room. After a couple of attempts with my keycard, the light flashed green and I pushed the door open. At last, home away from home.

The room was gorgeous, decorated in shades of beige and gold, with a few accents of red artistically tossed about. The furnishings were a little over the top, but I wasn't about to complain.

First things first. I found the thermostat and cranked up the air. The motor kicked on. Nice. A sigh eased from me. Next, unpacking. Some people lived out of their suitcases when they traveled. Not me. I needed to nest—make the room my own.

I unzipped my suitcase and pulled out my cosmetic bags—yes, I had two. Like my clothes, I hadn't been able to pare down the contents and I'd ended up dumping all my girl supplies into my bags. Better safe than sorry. I strode into the large bathroom and began unpacking my arsenal of beauty paraphernalia. Makeup, perfume, and lotion lined the sink like tiny soldiers, ready for any cosmetic mission.

I picked up the fancy soap provided by the hotel. A list of organic products went into making the luxury bar: oatmeal, avocado, olive oil. I didn't know whether to bathe with it or eat it. I gathered all the products and tossed them into my cosmetic bag, hoping tomorrow the maid would replenish my supply. By the time I went back to Alaska, I'd be fat with luxury hotel products. Did I mention I might have hording tendencies?

Sounds from the hall drew my attention. Leaning my head

out of the bathroom, I listened. Someone was talking—or loudly slurring—directly outside my room. I inched forward and pressed my eye to the peephole. A head full of blond curls swayed into view. I couldn't see if there were more people with her, but no doubt the woman was drunk and probably trying to find her room.

As quietly as possible, I folded the safety latch over the door. It was doubtful the drunken woman could get in, but I wasn't taking any chances. On and on she mumbled about finding her key, tottering back and forth. She was persistent, I'd give her that much.

How long was she going to stand there, fumbling and blocking my door? Eventually I'd have to leave. When I pressed my eye to the hole again, the woman looked up. For a split second her image wavered and then she chirped, "Beep, beep."

Before the information registered and I could jump back, the blonde stumbled through the solid door—and passed through me. An icy chill sliced to my bones. Doubling over, I spun to face the ghost.

"What the hell?" I glared at her and slowly uncoiled my body. "This is my room."

The blonde staggered, raising her translucent arms out to her sides. Her body swayed right and left until finding her balance. Then she straightened and slowly turned toward me, holding up her index finger. "I beg to differ with you, madam." She pointed a garish neon pink fingernail at her chest, stumbled back a few steps, and then righted herself. "This has been my room since New

Year's Eve, 2000."

"Really?" Another icy shudder rippled through me. "You've been haunting this room for over fifteen years?"

She wobbled, and glowered at me. "Haunting?"

Crap. I hated when ghosts didn't know they were dead. Informing them that they'd passed on was like telling people their loved one had died. Only in this case the loved one was her. "Yeah, I hate to be the bearer of bad news but..." I took a deep breath and plunged forward. "You're dead."

She stared at me for a few seconds and then burst out laughing. "I know I'm dead, silly." An instant later she sobered. "Wait. How can you see me?" She tilted her chin down and pinned me with a stare. "Are you dead, too?"

"No." I rubbed my arms, trying to scrub away the lingering effects of getting body-slammed by a spirit. "I'm a grim reaper."

"Cooool." The word leaked out of her like air escaping a balloon.

"Yeah, cool, but we have a problem." Not chancing more contact, I stepped into the bathroom doorway, dearly hoping she would leave. "I'm here for the next week. So, either you let me help you cross over, or you find somewhere else to hang for the next seven days." I gave her a placating smile. "Okay?"

"Yeah," she said, waving her finger at me. "That's not gonna happen." After an ungraceful pivot, she made an unsteady beeline for the bed—my bed, and flopped down on it, patting the comforter. "But…" She closed her eyes. "There's plenty of room for both of us." Again, her eyelids popped open. "Do you snore?"

"Not that I know of." I moved to the side of the bed, staring down at her. "Why are you drunk? Are you always wasted?" I'd never encountered an intoxicated spirit, and had assumed everybody converted to a non-inebriated state when they passed away. "Were you drunk when you died?"

"Gin and tonics, no, and yes." Slowly, she rolled to her stomach and rested her head on her hands. "I've been at a party."

"A ghost party?"

"I'm not sure." She furrowed her brow. "I mean, there were ghosts, but also living people." Her confusion melted and a dreamy smile spread across her face. "It was in this guy's suite upstairs. He's amazing."

"Is he a ghost?" I'd never heard of the dead and living mingling at a party, but what did I know about the afterlife, except that there was one? "Cuz, maybe you could stay with him."

Her eyes drifted shut again. "I don't think Big C is dead."

"Big C?"

"Yeah, the hottie who threw the party."

I didn't even want to know why they called him Big C. A quiet snore resonated from the spirit. "Hey." I nudged the bed with my knee. "What's your name?"

"Tandy," she whispered before sinking back into a drunken snore.

"Great." I glared at her for a few seconds and then whirled and stomped to the bathroom. Why had I actually entertained the notion that this week might be relaxing? Or at the very least, that I'd have my own room? "It frickin' figures."

I finger-combed my short, platinum hair and then spritzed it with hairspray. After that I flicked a coat of mascara along my lashes, then brushed my teeth. Standing back, I assessed my reflection. With only thirty minutes to primp, this was as good as it got. I retrieved my purse and room key, tossing Tandy a final glare. Hopefully she'd be gone by the time I got back.

No way was I sharing my room with a spectral party girl for seven days. If that meant hunting down Big C and pawning Tandy off on him, then that's exactly what I'd do.

About the Author

I'm thrilled every time a reader tells me they love my books, because it means I've done my job and connected with them. *Maybe a character resonates with them, or I've pushed the envelope a bit and wrote a scene they always wanted to read. Whatever the reason, that's why I write.*

I've been writing fulltime for five years, which isn't long for some, and a lifetime for others, but I've learned a couple of things about myself. I love to spoil my readers. I want them to get lost in my stories, even if it's only during their lunch break. And I want to make them laugh. It might only be a little in one of my medieval fantasies, or a lot from my Grim Reality Series. Humor is a big part of my life, the way I deal with problems, how I celebrate and have a good time, and approach raising my twin teenage daughters (Lord knows I need it when it comes to those two). I hope you become part of my family of readers, and I can help you forget your cares for a while and make you laugh.

To find out more about Boone Brux, visit the following sites:

- Facebook:facebook.com/BooneBruxAuthor
- Twitter: twitter.com/boonebrux
- Website: boonebrux.com
- Pinterest: pinterest.com/boonebrux
- Instagram: Instagram.com/boonebrux

Be part of an elite team and enjoy members only gifts such as free ebooks, first notice of sales, private contests, peeks into Boone's life, and so much more.

Join at: **smarturl.it/VIPClub**

If you enjoyed **To Catch Her Death**

☠ Tell your friends!!!

☠ Review the book on Amazon, Barnes & Noble, or Goodreads.

☠ Lend it. Share it with people you think would enjoy Boone's work.

18137952R00154

Printed in Poland
by Amazon Fulfillment
Poland Sp. z o.o., Wrocław